BOOK EIGHT IN THE LANDON SAGA

WARPATH

A SOLSTICE WESTERN

TELL COTTEN

1

Warpath

Tell Cotten

The Landon Saga novels by Tell Cotten

Confessions of a Gunfighter
Entwined Paths
Cooper
Rondo
Yancy
Lee
They Rode Together
Warpath

Also by Tell Cotten
Wanted: A Western Story Collection
(Includes a Landon Saga short story)

Dedication
To Ray and Ann
'Gargar' and 'Nina'

Illustrator: Bill Olivas
www.billolivas.com
wbolivas@yahoo.com

Cover Art:
Marcy Meinke/Converse Printing & Design
www.ConversePrinting.com
mike@converseprinting.com

Publisher's Note:

Solstice Publishing - www.solsticepublishing.com

While WARPATH can be read as a stand alone, it is recommended that new readers start with the first book in the series, CONFESSIONS OF A GUNFIGHTER.

The Landon Saga currently has four main characters that interact through the novels. For a quick reminder, below is the recent status of these characters.

Rondo Landon: Married to Rachel, Mr. Tomlin's daughter. Rondo is an ex-outlaw and lawman, now working for J.T. Tussle as a ranch hand.

Yancy Landon: Cousin to Rondo. Newly appointed as a Texas Ranger, and is romantically involved with Jessica Tussle, who is J.T. Tussle's niece.

Cooper Landon: Cousin to Rondo, and Yancy's older brother. Married to Josie, and has an adopted son, Wyatt, who was rescued from the Apaches. Like Yancy, he is also a newly appointed Texas Ranger.

Lee Mattingly: An ex-outlaw, and a friend of Rondo's. Romantically involved with April Gibson. He also owns part interest in The Palace Hotel, along with partner Brian Clark.

Part One
"The Attack"

Chapter one

The time had finally arrived.

It had been a six-month wait for No Worries, and his warriors were eager for blood.

No Worries was a young war chief of the Apaches, and he led his growing band with a ruthless recklessness. His name had become a household name, right up there with Geronimo.

He was tall for an Apache, standing at nearly six feet. He was very tan, and he had black hair with a muscled torso.

They had been traveling for weeks, riding southeast from their camp in the mountains in the New Mexico Territory.

They were now close to Empty-lake, Texas, just west of the Tomlin's ranch headquarters.

No Worries had never raided this deep into Texas. Mostly, Apaches roamed the New Mexico and Arizona Territories, and they also raided down south into Mexico.

It was now the morning of the raid, and the braves in camp watched No Worries for the signal to move out.

No Worries sat by himself, a blanket wrapped around his shoulders, deep in thought.

They had carefully scouted the surrounding area the day before, and he had scouts scattered in all directions to warn them if any riders were spotted.

They had also scouted the Tomlin's headquarters, and No Worries had been pleased when a young, dark headed woman was spotted.

She was the reason they were here.

Half a year ago, an Indian trader had come to their summer camp up in the mountains. He led several mules, packed with crates carrying rifles and ammunition.

No Worries usually traded pelts, but the Indian trader said no.

"What do you want?" No Worries asked, speaking in Apache.

"My boss, Ike Nash, has a strong enemy," the Indian trader, also speaking in Apache, replied. "He is also *your* enemy. His name is Landon."

"Landon," No Worries repeated the name.

"If they can, they will stop us from trading. No more rifles."

No Worries grunted at that.

"We must stop them," the Indian trader continued.

"How?"

"Kill them. *All* of them."

No Worries grunted again and nodded.

"But, the Landons are well respected by most white men," the Indian trader said. "It would look bad if Ike started a war against them."

"I have heard this name, Landon," No Worries declared, and his eyes glowed with hate. "It would be a great victory."

"It would," the Indian trader agreed. "And in return, Ike will give you these rifles. And many more after it's done."

"How?"

"Rondo Landon has a young, dark headed wife," he explained. "If you capture her and bring her to the mountains, the Landons will come."

A thoughtful look crossed No Worries' face, and he nodded his agreement.

"Ike would like you to wait several months," the Indian trader instructed, and explained, "Rondo killed Ike's son, Tanner, a while back. Ike wants Rondo to get comfortable with his new wife, so he will feel the same pain Ike felt when he lost Tanner."

No Worries was silent as he thought it over. He didn't care when it happened, just as long as he got more rifles.

9

"It is done," he declared.

"Ike will be pleased," the Indian trader replied. "Now, I have a map to show you the way."

The map contained detailed directions. And now, half a year later, they were here, camped a few miles from Tomlin's headquarters.

A coyote howling in the distance interrupted No Worries' thoughts. He stood, tossed his blanket aside, looked at his men, and gestured.

It was time.

Chapter two

It was a Saturday.

April Gibson worked at The Palace Hotel in Empty-lake. Mostly, she cooked, cleared tables, washed dishes, swept floors, and cleaned the rooms.

She was a tall, graceful looking woman with tired eyes and a wisp of natural gray hair here and there. She was in her early thirties.

Her new boss, Jeremiah Wisdom, had graciously given her most weekends off.

She knew the motive behind his kindness. He had feelings for her, and every weekend he invited her to accompany him on a picnic or a ride out into the country.

She had actually gone with him a few times, and she enjoyed their outings. But then Jeremiah brought up the subject of marriage, and since then she had politely refused his invitations. Instead, most Saturdays she rode out and visited her new friend, Rachel Landon.

This Saturday was no different. She and her daughter, June, saddled up at daylight and rode out to the Tomlin's headquarters.

June was ten years old. She had long, blond hair, round blue eyes, and a small, shapely face.

As always, the Tomlin's ranch headquarters was impressive. The main house was long and big, and the pole corrals were well kept and in good shape, as was the barn and bunkhouse.

June had recently become friends with the young, ranch hand Rory Wheeler.

As soon as they arrived, June dismounted, tied her horse to the railing, and ran toward the bunkhouse in search of Rory. Last week he had taught her the game of marbles, and she was eager to play again.

"Don't cause any trouble," April called after her.

"Yes, ma'am," June replied, and April smiled as she disappeared around the corner of the main house.

It pleased her that June and Rory had sprouted a friendship. Until now, June had been depressed and quiet ever since Lee had left.

Rachel came out of the house, and she and April greeted each other.

Rachel was in her early twenties. She had long, brown hair with sandy looking freckles that covered her face. She also had a knowing smile that always made her husband, Rondo, squirm.

"What do you want to do today?" Rachel asked.

"As long as I'm not cooking or washing dishes, I don't care," April replied.

Rachel smiled and asked, "Want to go for a ride?"

"I'd like that."

"I'll saddle a horse," Rachel said.

April nodded and followed her to the barn.

Chapter three

"Which direction should we ride today?" Bob Sprutt asked
Lucy Nash.

It was early morning, and Bob had just saddled two
horses and led them up to the main house.

They were on a ranch just south of the Tomlin's spread.
And, like most Saturdays, Bob was about to take Lucy out
riding and show her more of the ranch.

She wrinkled her nose in thought. She could feel Bob
watching her, and she liked the attention.

"Show me the north end today," she finally decided.

"Yes, ma'am," Bob drawled.

She giggled as he helped her get mounted. Next, he
stepped up on his horse, and they left in a trot.

Lucy's newly acquired dog was lying in the shade
beside the porch, and he bounded to his feet and followed.

"Is it all right if Precious comes along?" Lucy asked.

"Precious?" Bob raised an eyebrow.

"That's what I named him."

Bob forced himself not to smile.

"I don't see why not," he said.

Lucy grinned, and she looked back at her dog.

"Come along, Precious."

Lucy Nash was the half owner of the ranch. She was
young, very beautiful, and had long, blond hair.

Bob was a tall, thin fellow with blue eyes and light,
sandy hair. He was good with a Colt, and he was keen and
educated.

He was also an expert in forgery.

Butch Nelson, Lucy's partner, had been gone for several
weeks. He had left with the intent of an ill-advised attack
on J.T. Tussle's ranch up north, and he hadn't been heard
from since.

Lucy had specific orders to stay on the ranch, and she had quickly become bored. But then, a few weeks back, Bob had offered to show her the ranch, and these outings had become a welcome distraction.

Bob had also given her the dog with hopes of sprouting a friendship. So far, it was working.

They rode in silence for an hour.

The country around them was mainly rolling hills with a few trees, and there were also a few creeks spread about. The grass was tall and green, and their horses couldn't help but nip at it.

"Is it always this green?" Lucy asked as they pulled up at a creek.

"Not always," Bob replied as he dismounted and helped her down. "We've had more rain this year than normal."

He tied their horses to some nearby trees. Meanwhile, Precious loped off to explore some bushes across the creek.

Bob joined Lucy at the creek. She had sat on a log, and she looked thoughtful as she took in the view.

"We need more cows," she said.

"A lot more," Bob agreed as he sat beside her.

"Butch should be here, tending to things," Lucy said, and Bob could hear the discontent in her voice.

"Yes, ma'am."

"Do you think something happened to him?"

"It's possible."

"He's long overdue," Lucy pointed out.

Bob nodded thoughtfully.

"I know."

"I don't think he's coming back," Lucy said matter-of-factly.

"We don't know that," Bob argued.

Lucy turned suddenly and looked him in the eyes.

"You want him to come back?" She asked.

Bob was startled by the question.

"Well, sure, I guess. Don't you?"

"You haven't enjoyed my company?"

"Sure I have," Bob said quickly.

"If Butch comes back, our visits will come to an end," Lucy pointed out.

"I know that," Bob said, almost wistfully.

"Well then?"

Bob took in a big breath, exhaled, and shook his head.

"I guess not," he said with a sheepish smile.

"With Butch gone, that makes me the full owner," Lucy said. "But, I'm also a woman."

"You sure are."

"I'll need help. Running a ranch is a lot of work."

"It sure is."

"Are you interested?"

"In becoming your partner?"

"Yes."

Hope filled Bob's face as he looked at her.

"You know I am."

Lucy smiled coyly, and Bob's heart skipped a beat.

Chapter four

Their horses were fresh and full of energy. April and Rachel gave them their heads, and they trotted south at a brisk pace.

Both girls enjoyed the ride and the freedom of being away from others.

They finally pulled up next to some tall, cottonwood trees. They dismounted, tied their horses to some tree branches, and took a walk across a green, majestic looking meadow.

Before they left, Rachel pulled out her rifle and cradled it in her arms.

"Is that necessary?" April's eyes twinkled.

"You've lived in town too long," Rachel chided her friend. "You never know when you might walk up on a snake, or something worse."

"What's worse than a snake?"

"Something with two legs."

April laughed. They walked a bit more, and she sighed wistfully as she took in the view.

"It's so beautiful here," she stated. "It's hard to believe anything bad could be lurking about."

"I've always thought this little meadow would be an ideal spot for a house," Rachel said.

"It would," April agreed, and she shot her friend a curious look. "Have you and Rondo discussed it?"

"We don't have the money," Rachel shrugged, and added, "Maybe someday. But right now, Rondo is just hoping for a ranch job with J.T. Tussle. We sure need it."

"I'm sure he'll get the job."

"He'd better," Rachel said, and suddenly she looked worried. "I can't figure what's taking him so long. He should have returned weeks ago."

"I'm sure he's fine," April tried to reassure her.

Rachel didn't look convinced as they walked along. A few minutes passed, and she cleared her throat.

"As soon as Rondo gets back, I'll have news for him," she said, her eyes wide and bright.

"Oh?"

Rachel smiled but didn't say anything.

"Rachel Landon! Are you going to have a baby?"

Rachel nodded, still smiling, and her face flushed with excitement.

"Congratulations," April grinned, and asked, "Rondo has no idea?"

"No. I wasn't sure myself until a few days ago."

"Who else knows?"

"Only you," Rachel replied, and explained, "I don't want anyone else to know until Rondo does. And, if I told my parents, *everyone* would know within the week."

"I won't tell," April promised. A few seconds passed, and she asked, "Do you think Rondo will be surprised?"

"I'm sure he will be," Rachel answered. "We've been so busy these past few months, we haven't even discussed children."

"He'll be overjoyed."

"I hope so."

"Of course, he might not show it," April warned. "Men are like that."

"I know," Rachel murmured.

April smiled. But then a thought occurred to her, and her smile faded.

"I saw Rondo in town, right before he left," she announced as she changed the subject.

"You did?"

"He said it was a strong possibility that he might run into Lee."

"Yes, that was partly why he left, was to warn him and Brian about Rock Bullen," Rachel recalled.

April nodded, and her face looked strained.

17

It was no secret that April had strong feelings for Lee Mattingly. But then, Lee had killed a politician in self-defense. He had to leave town, and he hadn't been seen since.

"I wonder if Rondo found him?" April asked.

"I'm sure he did," Rachel replied. "My father told me Rondo could track a shadow in the dark."

April smiled faintly and said, "I asked him to deliver a message."

"Oh?" Rachel raised an inquisitive eyebrow.

"I wanted Lee to know that June prays every night for him to come back."

"Does she?"

"Yes," April said. She hesitated, and added quietly, "So do I."

Rachel felt sorry for her friend. A few seconds passed, and she asked, "Does Lee know how you feel?"

"I think he does."

"Well then, he'll show up one of these days," Rachel declared.

"I'm not so sure. Why, he's probably forgotten all about us by now," April said sullenly, and she took in a deep breath and sighed.

Rachel couldn't think of anything comforting to say, and neither one said anything for a moment.

"I've been spending some time with Jeremiah Wisdom," April said suddenly.

"Yes, I know."

"But, I haven't seen him in a few weeks. In fact, I've been avoiding him."

"Why?"

"He keeps mentioning marriage."

"And what did you tell him?"

"That I would think about it."

"And have you?"

"Yes," April said. She paused, and added, "I know he has a past. But, he seems to be trying hard. He's been good and decent to me, and he's also kind to June."

"But you don't love him," Rachel pointed out.

"I don't," April agreed. "But, there's more to consider than just my feelings."

"Such as?"

"June," April replied. "She's had it rough these last few years. She lost her father *and* sister. She deserves to be happy."

"And marrying Jeremiah would do that?" Rachel frowned, not convinced.

"We'd be a family again."

"What about Lee?" Rachel reminded.

"Lee's just a dream. But Jeremiah is real."

"Dreams come true, sometimes," Rachel replied. "Before we were married, Rondo left on a cattle drive, and he told me he wasn't coming back. But, I said I would wait for him, and I did. He finally came back, and so will Lee."

"You really think so?" April looked wistful.

"Yes," Rachel declared. "I do."

Chapter five

Craig Tomlin had white hair, and his face was weathered and wrinkled. But his eyes were clear and sharp, and he never seemed to miss a thing.

He was in his late fifties, and he had lived a full life. He had been on numerous cattle drives, fought rustlers and Indians, and had suffered through several West Texas droughts. Nothing much surprised the old cattleman anymore.

He felt uneasy as he and Buster went down to the barn to do the morning chores. He didn't know what it was, but he sensed that something was wrong.

He studied the landscape with care, and he narrowed his eyes.

It was still, and very quiet.

Too quiet, he thought.

There were no birds chirping, no nothing. There was only an eerie silence, and he felt the hairs on the back of his neck start to stand.

Buster came out of the barn, carrying a pail of milk. He was walking toward the main house, but he stopped when he noticed Mr. Tomlin.

"Something wrong?" He asked.

"Where's Rachel and April?" Mr. Tomlin asked.

"They rode out."

Concern filled Mr. Tomlin's face.

"How long ago?"

"'Bout an hour," Buster replied, and asked, "What is it, Mr. Tomlin?"

"Not sure yet," Mr. Tomlin replied. A few seconds passed, and he added, "Stop at the bunkhouse and grab your rifle before going up to the main house."

Buster looked thoughtful.

"Yes, sir," he said, and took off.

Mr. Tomlin studied the landscape once more, and then he trailed after Buster.

He found Rory and June in front of the bunkhouse. They were on their hands and knees, playing a game of marbles.

Mr. Tomlin smiled faintly as he watched June. Her face was flushed and excited as she waited for her turn.

He cleared his throat, and they looked up at him.

"Who's winning?" He asked.

"I am," June declared.

He smiled again and nodded.

"Let's move the game up to the main house," he suggested.

He kept his voice casual, but Rory noticed the concerned look on his face.

"Is something wrong?" Rory asked.

"Could be. Not sure yet."

Rory was curious, but he didn't ask anymore questions. While Mr. Tomlin stood there keeping watch, they gathered up the marbles.

"Best bring your rifle along," Mr. Tomlin told Rory.

"Yes, sir."

Mr. Tomlin waited while he hurried inside the bunkhouse. Moments later he returned with his rifle, and they all went up to the main house.

A chirping sound was heard in the distance as Mr. Tomlin shut and bolted the front door.

Chapter six

"So, how's the paperwork coming?" Lucy Nash asked Bob. "Is my name Jenny yet?"

"Not yet."

"What's the holdup?" Lucy frowned impatiently.

"No holdup. It just takes time," Bob replied, and added, "Don't worry. You'll be Jenny before you know it."

"I hope so," Lucy said wistfully, and it fell silent as they sat there thinking their own thoughts.

Lucy had done a lot of dishonest things in her life. Most recently, she had escaped from Huntsville prison. She was determined not to go back, and changing her name was the easiest way to put her past behind her once and for all.

"Jenny Sprutt," she said thoughtfully, and she smiled coyly at Bob. "Sounds pleasant, doesn't it?"

Bob looked startled.

"Sprutt? That's my last name."

"I know that."

"Are you wanting to be known as my sister, or as something else?"

"'Something else' might be more fun."

Bob stared at her.

"You sure are direct," he said.

"I know what I want," she shrugged.

"Meaning me?"

"Yes," Lucy said matter-of-factly, and added, "You seem surprised."

"I reckon I am."

"Bob," Lucy said patiently. "When a woman is offering to marry you, don't overthink it. Just say yes."

"Yes, ma'am," Bob grinned.

"Well then, we'd best be heading back," she suggested.

They stood and headed toward their horses.

"Where's Precious?" Lucy asked suddenly.

"I saw him over there in those bushes a while ago," Bob pointed across the creek. "I'll fetch him."

"Thank you, Bob."

He nodded and started across the shallow creek.

He had just reached the far bank when he heard the dog start to bark furiously. A few seconds later, the bark turned into an agonizing howl.

"What's going on?" Lucy asked, concerned.

"Something's after your dog!" Bob hollered back. "Cat, more than likely."

He turned, sprinted back across the creek, and hurried over to his horse.

"Precious!" Lucy cried, and she ran towards the high-pitched howl.

"Lucy, wait!"

She ignored the warning as she ran on. Bob shouted after her once more, and then he pulled his rifle from his scabbard and hurried after her.

There was a clearing between them and the bushes, and Lucy was halfway across it when loud, terrifying yells sounded out.

Lucy halted in her tracks. That wasn't the sound of a cat; that was a human sound.

Before she could react, four Indians on horses came riding out of the bushes. They held wooden clubs.

They were shirtless, their faces were painted, and they wore ornamented breechcloths with buckskin leggings. They looked terrifying as they ran their ponies straight at her.

There was a yell from behind, but she ignored it as she stared at the oncoming riders. She was so scared she couldn't move.

She heard a rifle shot, and then the first Indian reached her.

He swung his club and struck her in the side of the head. It was a solid blow, and a stream of blood burst from her scalp.

Lucy hit the ground face first. She groaned and passed out as the other Indians rode by her.

Bob was still firing his rifle, but his frantic shots didn't hit any of them.

He dropped his rifle in fright and stumbled backwards as they reached him. He fell on his back, and he screamed in terror as they rode in a circle around him, clubbing him to death.

Lucy was still unconscious as the Indians rode back to her and dismounted. They squatted beside her, and she was unaware as curious fingers reached out and felt her curly, blond hair.

Chapter seven

"Did you hear that?" Rachel stopped and cocked her head sideways.

They were halfway across the meadow, heading back to their horses.

"No," April replied. "What was it?"

"I thought I heard rifle shots. To the south."

"I didn't hear it," April said, and added, "But, you're younger than I am. You can probably hear better too."

"You aren't that old," Rachel chided.

"No, but I'm not getting any younger."

"Neither am I," Rachel reminded.

They walked on, and Rachel suddenly noticed how quiet it was. She sensed that something was wrong, and she quickened her pace.

She was several feet in front of April when they reached the horses.

Both horses were spooked, and their ears were pointed forward as they snorted at something in the bushes.

Rachel was about to say something when she heard April gasp, followed by a terrifying scream.

Rachel instinctively brought her rifle up and spun around.

The fiercest looking Indian she had ever seen stood in front of her. His face was covered with war paint, and he was swinging a wooden club.

Before she could pull the trigger, a hard blast hit her in the side of the face. There was an explosion in her head, and then she felt nothing else.

***

When Rachel regained consciousness, her head throbbed. She could also smell a rank odor, and it made her nauseous.

She didn't want to open her eyes, but her body was swaying, and it was very uncomfortable.

Only one eye would work. The other eye was swelling, and wouldn't respond. She blinked her good eye several times, and her vision slowly cleared.

The first thing she saw was the ground. She was several feet above it, and several seconds passed before she realized that she was draped over her horse.

She tried to move, but couldn't. Her hands were tied together harshly with rawhide leather, and already her hands were swelling. Her feet were also tied, and she could tell that her hands and feet were lashed together underneath her horse so she wouldn't fall off.

She wondered if April was alive.

She couldn't see much from her position; just the horse and the ground. Her horse was being led, and she could make out the shadow of an Indian riding the horse in front of her.

She ached all over. Her head felt like it might explode, and she had trouble breathing.

She tried to lift her head, but couldn't. Next, she tried to free her hands, but the more she struggled the tighter the knots seem to get.

She finally gave up on her feeble efforts. She just lay there, drifting in and out of consciousness, as she felt her horse's muscles move underneath her.

Chapter eight

Rachel woke with a small jolt about an hour later.

Her body rolled forward as her horse went down a steep knoll. For a moment she thought she would slide off, but the Indians had tied her to her horse very skillfully.

She moaned in pain as they reached the bottom and leveled out. Her body rocked backwards against the seat of her saddle, and she ended up flat on her stomach.

They rode a bit further, and then they stopped abruptly. Rachel could smell campfire smoke, and she figured they had arrived at their camp.

She didn't dare move. Instead, she just lay there, breathing quick and shallow, as she heard footsteps approaching.

Unrecognizable Apache words reached her ears. And then, she felt a hard, dry hand grab her hair and twist cruelly.

She resisted the urge to cry out. Instead, she remained limp, her good eye clamped shut.

The Indian warrior lifted her head, and Rachel could feel his breath on her face as he looked at her.

His horrible odor almost caused her to vomit. But, she fought down the urge, all the while keeping her eye shut.

Suddenly, the Indian gave a loud cry of satisfaction. He released her hair, and her head dropped back down.

Rachel heard footsteps circling her horse. Moments later, she heard something being cut. And then, without warning, she was shoved from behind. She went flying off her horse, and she hit the ground face first.

She was stunned by the sudden fall. A groan escaped from her lips, and she welcomed the darkness as she passed out again.

Chapter nine

The agonizing pain in Rachel's shoulders and hands brought her back to her senses. Her wrists ached from the tight bonds, and her fingers were numb.

"Rachel, wake up," she heard a soft voice say. "Wake up. *Please.*"

She forced her good eye open, blinked a few times, and looked around.

She was on her back, stretched out beside a small campfire.

April was beside her, and Rachel forgot all about her aches and pains when she spotted her friend. April's face was pale, and she looked ill.

There was also another woman sprawled out beside April. She had an ugly welt on her head, and she looked dazed and confused.

Several Indians stood around the main campfire a small distance from them. They were talking in loud voices, and they sounded angry.

Rachel had never seen Indians this close, and she couldn't help but be fascinated.

They were a fierce looking bunch. Most were shirtless, and they had tan, muscular bodies. Only a few held bow and arrows; the rest were armed with rifles.

"Are they going to kill us?" April asked, her voice small and timid.

"I don't think so," Rachel whispered back, trying to comfort her friend. "We would already be dead if it was our scalps they were after."

"What will they do to us?"

"They'll probably take us back to their main camp," Rachel figured.

"And then?"

"I don't know. Make us wives, maybe."

A look of horror crossed April's face.

"God, please no!" She prayed.

"It's better than dying," Rachel pointed out.

The woman beside them heard their conversation, and she groaned as she came to her senses.

"Are you all right?" Rachel asked her.

"No!" She wailed.

"Keep your voice down!" Rachel hissed.

"Where are we?" She asked.

Rachel told her, and the woman's eyes grew wide when she spotted the Indians.

"Easy now; don't make any sudden movements," Rachel urged. "Don't let them know you're afraid."

She didn't reply, but she did manage to nod.

"I'm Rachel, and this is April. Who are you?"

"Lucy," she managed. "My name is Lucy."

"What happened to you?" Rachel asked. "How did you get here?"

Before Lucy could reply, the tallest Apache in the bunch knelt by the fire, grabbed something, straightened up, and walked towards them.

Lucy saw him approaching, and her eyes grew wide with terror, as did April's.

"Here they come!" Lucy wailed.

Chapter ten

Even Rachel couldn't help but tremble as the cruel looking Apache approached them.

He seemed to be their leader. His face was harsh, and his eyes were cold.

He held a chunk of meat in his hand, and Rachel was relieved to see it. Meat was better than a knife or a tomahawk.

He stopped in front of them, and it was silent as he studied them.

Tears streamed down Lucy and April's face, but Rachel forced herself not to cry. Instead, she stared back with defiance.

The Apache noticed this, and he grunted his approval.

Several tense seconds passed, and then the Apache spoke in broken English.

"Landon," he said, and nodded at Rachel.

A jolt of surprise passed through her.

"Yes," she said. "I am Rachel Landon."

He grunted again and nodded.

"Landon?" He asked, and pointed at April.

"Yes," Rachel said quickly. "She is also a Landon."

The Apache seemed pleased. He looked at Lucy and scowled.

"You, no Landon," he said.

"Yes, I am!" Lucy insisted. "I'm a Landon too!"

"You lie!" He narrowed his eyes.

"Please, don't kill me!" She wailed.

He ignored her as he looked back at Rachel.

"Me, No Worries," he said, and thumped his chest.

"I have heard of you," Rachel said truthfully. "You are a great war chief of the Apaches."

She wasn't sure if he had understood her. He stood there a moment more, looking back at Lucy, and his hand moved to his waist.

He pulled out a tomahawk, and Lucy's eyes grew wide as he walked toward her.

"Please, no!" She cried out.

He ignored her protests as he grabbed her by the hair and yanked her up to her knees. Lucy sobbed as he moved around behind her.

Even Rachel was surprised when he slashed her bonds, and then he walked over and cut her and April loose. Next, he tossed the meat down in front of them.

"Eat," he said roughly, and walked away.

All three immediately started rubbing their hands and arms. It took several minutes to get the blood flowing, and it was a painful process.

"We'd best do as he says," Rachel said as she picked up the meat. "There's no telling when we might eat again."

April nodded solemnly, and Rachel tried to look cheerful as she divided up the meat as evenly as possible.

"This is a good sign," Rachel said as she bit into the meat and tore off a piece with her teeth.

"Why's that?" April asked.

"They wouldn't be giving us food if they planned on killing us."

April and Lucy nodded in agreement as they began chewing.

"This tastes horrible," April made a face. "What is it?"

Rachel didn't reply. Instead, she gestured at the main campfire.

April and Lucy looked, and their eyes grew wide when they spotted the remains of a dog.

"Precious!" Lucy cried softly.

Chapter eleven

It took awhile, but they finally managed to choke down their food. Afterwards, Rachel took a careful look around camp.

She was startled when she spotted five limp bodies laid out on the ground across the camp. All five were Indians, and they were dead.

Acting nonchalant, she counted the Indians in camp. Her final count came to twenty-one.

Camp was busy, and to Rachel it looked like they were preparing to leave. Her suspicions were confirmed when they picked up the dead Indians and draped them over their ponies.

"Why are they taking them with us?" April whispered.

"I remember Pa say that Indians rarely leave their dead," Rachel whispered back. "They'll probably bury them in a day or two, when they're sure no one will find them."

"I wonder how they died?"

"They probably attacked the ranch headquarters."

"June!" April's eyes grew wide with concern. "Do you suppose-."

"Pa's fought Indians before," Rachel interrupted. "I'm sure they're fine. Besides, if the raid had been a success, we would see scalps."

"Look!" April pointed.

There, hanging from a horse, was a fresh scalp. From what they could tell, the hair was light and sandy.

"That's Bob," Lucy spoke up, her voice low and sullen.

"Who's Bob?" Rachel asked.

"He was with me when they attacked," Lucy explained. "We had just become engaged."

"I'm sorry," Rachel said.

Lucy snorted, but didn't reply.

"I wonder how that Indian knew your last name?" April changed the subject.

"I have no idea," Rachel replied.

"Seems odd."

"Very," Rachel agreed.

"What do we do now?"

"We stay alive," Rachel declared.

"How do we do that?"

"By not being a problem," Rachel said, and added, "Whatever happens, don't show fear. Pa said Indians hate cowards."

April nodded.

"Anything else?"

Rachel paused while she recalled her father's words.

"Don't complain about anything," she finally said, and added, "Sooner or later they'll be coming for us, and we just have to hang on until they find us."

"Who's that?" Lucy looked up.

"My husband," Rachel said matter-of-factly.

"And who is your husband?"

"Rondo Landon."

Lucy snorted again and shook her head.

"You can wait for miracles if you want. First chance I get, I'm getting out of here," she declared.

"How do you plan on doing that?" Rachel scowled at her.

"By staying watchful and alert," Lucy said. "You wait and see. An opportunity will present itself. It always does."

"Even if you managed to escape, then what?" Rachel argued. "We're a long ways from any town, and it would be impossible to outrun them."

Lucy didn't reply, and several seconds passed.

Rachel frowned and started to say something. However, she stopped herself when she saw No Worries walking towards them.

"We go," he said roughly.

33

They got to their feet. He motioned for them to follow, and they headed towards the horses.

Chapter twelve

Rachel was relieved when they were allowed to ride their horses the normal way. However, the Apaches still tied their hands to the saddle horn, and they led their horses.

No Worries was in front, and he rode in a brisk trot, heading northwest.

Rachel was extremely sore, and the bouncing in the saddle didn't help any. With her hands tied, it was difficult to find any rhythm, and her body took a beating.

Rachel recalled that her Pa had said Indians were cruel to their horses, and she found this to be true. They kept up a grueling pace, and hour after hour passed.

Rachel figured they would stop when darkness hit, but she was wrong. They never broke stride, and they rode under a full moon.

Along towards morning, they finally stopped at a creek.

All the horses were lathered in sweat, and they wanted to drink deeply. However, the Apaches wisely only allowed them to drink for short moments at a time.

To Rachel's dismay, they weren't allowed to dismount. Instead, an Apache brought them a gourd filled with water. They opened their mouths, and he poured some water in.

The water was cool and pleasant. Rachel yearned for more, but the Apache walked away after only a few swallows.

Rachel was grateful they had stopped. She ached all over, and she couldn't help but wince as she stretched in the saddle.

"There they go, taking the dead Indians," April said, and she gestured with her head.

Some color had returned to April's face, and Rachel was glad that her friend's voice no longer trembled.

Rachel looked, and several Indians were riding off, leading behind them the horses carrying their dead companions.

"Do you think they'll bury them now?" April asked.

"Probably so," Rachel figured.

The Apaches returned an hour or so later, without their dead. They led the extra Indian ponies behind them.

No Worries gestured for everybody to mount up, and they took off again in a brisk trot, traveling northwest.

Chapter thirteen

They traveled almost nonstop for two days, all the while keeping up the grueling pace.

Three horses collapsed from exhaustion, but that didn't bother the Apaches. They now had five extra horses, so they just cut the horses' throats and climbed on the next one.

A deep hunger gnawed in the pit of Rachel's stomach, and April and Lucy looked exhausted. But, all three managed to carry themselves with poise and bravery.

By now, Rachel could see the mountains of the New Mexico Territory in the far distance. However, the country around them was mainly flat, with a few rolling hills.

The terrain had turned dry and bare, without much grass or cover. It was also hot, and Rachel's battered clothes were drenched with sweat.

Another horse collapsed at the end of the second day.

They were close to a small tank filled with rainwater, so No Worries signaled for them to stop. He grunted a few commands, and everyone hustled about as they prepared camp.

The women were escorted off to the side, and the Apache watching them gestured for them to sit. They did, and then they stretched their cramped muscles.

Meanwhile, another Indian slit the downed horse's throat, finishing the job. Other Indians came up beside the horse, and their knives flashed as they skillfully cut out some meat.

By the time they were through, a fire had been built.

As soon as the meat was cooked, No Worries cut out a chunk and brought it over to them. He dropped it at Rachel's feet, made a motion to eat, and returned to the main fire.

Rachel picked up the meat and split it between them as best as she could.

Hungry as she was, Rachel still almost gagged when she tasted the tough and stringy horsemeat. But, she resisted the urge, chewed, and swallowed.

April was watching her.

"How is it?" She asked.

"Better than Precious," Rachel replied.

Chapter fourteen

"Just look at them," Lucy said, and her voice filled with scorn. "They're gorging themselves."

Rachel nodded in agreement. The Indians had gathered around the main campfire, and she had never seen anyone eat so much, so fast.

"It might be days before we eat again," Rachel explained.

"As much as they're eating, they'll probably sleep hard tonight," Lucy figured.

"So will I," April admitted. "I'm exhausted."

"Do you think they'll tie us up tonight?" Lucy asked.

"I doubt it," Rachel reasoned. "They're probably not worried about us escaping, this far out."

Lucy looked thoughtful. It was silent a moment, and she stood abruptly.

"What are you doing?" Rachel hissed.

"Trying something."

Before Rachel could reply, Lucy walked boldly toward the dirt tank.

The Indian guarding them watched curiously, but he remained still.

Lucy walked to the edge of the dirt tank. She knelt down, cupped her hands, and dipped up several mouthfuls of water.

When she'd had her fill, she straightened up and walked back to Rachel and April.

"Did you see that?" Lucy boasted as she sat back down. "They didn't stop me."

"You weren't trying to escape," Rachel retorted.

"I will be next time."

Rachel frowned, but didn't reply. Instead, she looked at April.

"Thirsty?"

"Yes, very much."

"Let's get a drink then," Rachel suggested, and they stood and walked towards the dirt tank.

***

After their meal, the Apaches relaxed around the campfire.

They didn't talk. Instead, they just sat there and stared out into the darkness.

Lucy looked anxious, but she still stretched out on the ground. After a moment Rachel could hear her breathing steadily, but she wasn't convinced that she was asleep.

Tired as she was, Rachel didn't think on it long. She and April stretched out, and it didn't take them long to fall asleep.

***

Hours later, a startling cry stirred Rachel and April. They were frightened, and they sat up abruptly.

The Apache keeping watch stood over them, and an astonished look was on his face.

Rachel glanced sideways, and her good eye grew wide.

Lucy was gone, and she could hear a horse running in the distance.

Camp was in chaos, and No Worries appeared with a tomahawk in hand. His eyes were harsh as he looked at Rachel and April, and then he turned to the Apache warrior.

Heated words were exchanged, and No Worries turned away abruptly. He grunted a few commands, and he and three other warriors ran over to the horses and mounted up. They kicked their horses unmercifully as they disappeared into the darkness.

Camp quieted down, and April glanced at Rachel.

"Lucy escaped!" She hissed.

"Looks like it," Rachel said.

"I can't believe she got away!"

"She hasn't yet," Rachel replied softly.

Chapter fifteen

No Worries returned a few hours later. He and his warriors dismounted in the darkness and walked up to the fire.

They talked in loud voices, and then No Worries approached April and Rachel.

He walked deliberately, and his face was emotionless.

April suddenly gasped, and her stomach heaved. She clamped a hand over her mouth and smothered a scream.

Hanging from No Worries' waist was a fresh, bloody scalp. There was no doubt that the long, curly blond hair was Lucy's.

Rachel sucked in her breath as No Worries stopped in front of them. A look of anger crossed his face as he glared at them.

He lifted the scalp from his waist and shook it at them.

April looked away as fresh blood dripped to the ground, but Rachel looked him boldly in the eyes.

"You run, you die," he said harshly.

"We understand," Rachel said, her voice low and solemn.

He grunted at that, scowled, and walked away.

"I can't do this anymore," April wailed, and her voice trembled.

"We don't have a choice," Rachel replied matter-of-factly.

"Why does it matter?" April argued. "Didn't you see the look in his eyes? He's going to kill us. It's just a matter of time."

"No, Lucy is dead because she was foolish," Rachel said. "We won't make the same mistake."

"Do you really think Rondo will come for us?"

"I do," Rachel replied, and added, "Lee Mattingly will be with him."

A few seconds passed as April thought on that, and she nodded slightly.

"All right," she said softly. "For June's sake, I'll hang on until they get here."

Rachel tried to smile encouragingly, and after that it was silent as they thought their own thoughts.

Where are you, Rondo? Rachel thought wistfully. *Do you even know what's happened to us?*

Rachel felt a cramp in her stomach, and the thought of her baby came to mind. She drew her knees to her stomach, wrapped her arms around her legs, and rested her chin on top of her knees.

Hang on, little one, she thought. *We'll survive. We have to. Rondo's coming for us, and I know it with all my heart.*

Part Two
"Bad News"

Chapter sixteen

They had been traveling for weeks. They were saddle worn, covered in dust, and in need of a bath and shave.

They made camp that night only a few miles from Empty-lake. They tended to their horses, gathered some wood, built a fire, and cooked supper.

There were five men in the group, plus a packhorse named No-see-ums and a pack mule named Jug-head.

Their names were Rondo, Yancy and Cooper Landon, Lee Mattingly, and Brian Clark.

Brian was the oldest. An ex-outlaw, he was a grizzled veteran in his mid-fifties. He was always careful; he never took any chances unless he had to.

Lee was also an ex-outlaw in his mid-thirties. He had a gentleman-like way about him, and he had a different set of ethics than most. He was soft spoken, and was loyal to those he considered friends.

Rondo Landon was perhaps the most famous ex-outlaw of the group, known as the man who killed Ben Kinrich. He wasn't proud of that, but it had to be done.

He was small and hard bodied, and he always displayed his ivory-handled Colt on his right hip.

Yancy and Cooper Landon were brothers, and both were newly appointed Texas Rangers.

Like his cousin Rondo, Yancy had a smaller build.

He was a very somber man. He never talked unless he had to, and when he did he was usually clear, certain, and to the point. He was also painfully honest, no matter the cost.

He was well respected for his skills with his Colt six-shooter. However, Cooper was just as dangerous.

Tall and wide shouldered, Cooper wasn't nearly as good with a Colt. Instead, his specialty was with his Henry rifle. He was real accurate with it, and mighty quick too. He had a special way of swinging it up, and he was almost as fast as Yancy's draw.

Cooper was also a very good tracker, as was Rondo.

Yancy and Cooper's first assignment as Texas Rangers was to crush the corrupt empire that Ike Nash had created. Ike was now dead, thanks to Lee Mattingly, and all but one had been brought to justice.

That last person was Lucy Nash, and they were traveling to Empty-lake to arrest her and send her back to Huntsville prison.

As for Rondo, he had a ranch job waiting in Midway. He was headed for Mr. Tomlin's headquarters to pick up Rachel.

Lee and Brian were on their way to Empty-lake to take ownership of their hotel.

Lee also planned on seeing a lady.

Named April.

Chapter seventeen

They turned in early that evening. Everyone was anxious to reach Empty-lake, and they planned on riding out at first light.

A few minutes passed. As usual, Brian was the first to fall asleep, and everyone could hear his loud snoring.

Yancy and Cooper had spread out their bedrolls across the camp from the others. Cooper sat up, glanced at Yancy, and sighed.

"This should be the last night we have to listen to *that*," Cooper said softly.

"Silence is my friend," Yancy agreed, and added wistfully, "I miss him."

"Me too," Cooper declared.

Yancy didn't reply. He was on his back, his hands clasped behind his head, as he looked up at the clear, dark sky.

"Beautiful, ain't they," he commented.

"What is?"

"The stars," Yancy explained. "They sure are bright tonight."

Cooper frowned. He studied his younger brother a moment and cleared his throat.

"You feeling all right?"

"Sure," Yancy nodded and looked at Cooper. "Why do you ask?"

"You've never talked about the stars before."

"So?"

"In fact, last time I mentioned the stars, you thought I was crazy."

"You think *I'm* crazy?"

"No, but ever since we left Tussle's headquarters, you sure been acting odd."

"How's that?"

"Tonight you didn't even pour sugar in your coffee," Cooper pointed out, and added, "And we have a full sack."

Yancy looked startled.

"I didn't?"

"Nope."

"Well, I must have forgotten. I've had a lot on my mind lately. That's all."

"And I know what's been on your mind," Cooper said, and declared, "Jessica Tussle."

Yancy scowled at that. He opened his mouth, but then closed it. A few seconds passed, and he smiled.

"I thought so," Cooper chuckled and leaned back.

It was silent for a moment. Yancy sat up while he tried to think, and Cooper just waited.

"Jessica is an interesting woman," Yancy finally said.

"Seems like," Cooper agreed.

"Soon as we take care of Lucy, think I'll ride back to Midway and marry her," Yancy declared.

Cooper was startled, and he shot Yancy a surprised look.

"What if she says no?"

"She won't."

"You seem confident."

"I am."

"What about your problems?"

"What problems?"

"You know. She's rich, and you ain't."

Yancy waved a hand at his brother.

"We worked that all out before we left. She's not as wealthy as you think."

"She seemed well off to me."

"Well, she's not. Not anymore."

"Where did her wealth go? Did she give it away?"

"Something like that."

"And that makes you happy."

"Does."

"Most men in your position would be happier if she was wealthy," Cooper pointed out.

"I'm not like most folks."

"You don't have to tell me that," Cooper smiled. He thought a moment, and added, "Our little house is going to be crowded."

"Been considering that," Yancy replied. "Judge Parker told me the Texas Rangers are planning on building a Ranger Station right there at Midway. There'll be living quarters in the back. Jessica and I can live there, and you, Josie, and Wyatt can have the house."

"You have this all figured out."

"You don't like it?"

"No, it should work," Cooper said, and he smiled as another thought occurred to him. "Does Sheriff Wagons know?" He asked.

"Not that I know of."

"He'll be thrilled, having you right next to him."

Yancy grunted at that, and Cooper's smile lingered.

"This'll be the first time we've lived apart since before the war," Cooper pointed out. "Take some getting used to."

"We can visit often."

Cooper chuckled, and Yancy joined in.

Before Cooper could reply, Lee Mattingly cleared his throat from across the camp.

"This conversation has been touching, but would you two wrap it up soon? Some of us are actually trying to sleep."

Yancy scowled. He started to reply harshly, but then decided against it. He nodded goodnight to Cooper, and it fell silent as he settled down into his bedroll.

Chapter eighteen

They were up before daylight. They rebuilt the fire, cooked breakfast and coffee, and ate. Afterwards, they rolled up their bedrolls and packed up camp.

Rondo and Lee looked anxious, and Brian grinned at them while they saddled their horses.

"You two look eager," he said, and their faces reddened slightly.

"I reckon I am," Rondo admitted. "I haven't seen Rachel in a long while."

Brian nodded and looked at Lee.

"You must be anxious to see Jeremiah Wisdom."

"What for?" Lee looked confused.

"You know. The hotel. We've got to get everything settled. Jeremiah isn't even aware that we're his new partners."

"Hotel can wait."

"Oh?" Brian tried to look surprised. "If not the hotel, then what is it?"

"You know."

"Reckon I do," Brian said, and grinned widely.

Lee tightened his cinch, turned, and noticed Brian's grin.

"You're enjoying seeing me suffer, ain't you," Lee scowled.

"Yes, I believe I am."

"Why?"

"Mebbe I'm rooting for you. And for April, and June."

"She might not even talk to me."

"I think she will," Brian replied, and added, "She'll be mighty glad to see you too."

Lee smiled at the thought.

Chapter nineteen

They were just about to climb on their horses when Cooper spotted some movement in the distance. There were also little puffs of dust in the air.

"Riders coming," he announced.

"How many?" Yancy asked as he walked up beside Cooper and squinted.

"'Bout a half dozen, give or take," Cooper replied, and added, "They seem to be in a hurry."

Yancy nodded in agreement, and they watched as the riders approached from the west.

"That's Ross Stewart in front," Rondo suddenly said.

"Yeah, and that's Jeremiah Wisdom behind him," Lee added.

"I wonder what he's doing out here?" Brian frowned his disapproval. "He should be in town, running our hotel."

"We'll find out soon enough," Lee replied.

As they got closer, they could tell that the horses were lathered in sweat, and the men's faces looked grim.

"It's early to be sweating like that," Cooper observed. "They must have ridden through the night."

"Trouble," Yancy said softly, and everyone nodded.

They rode up and halted in front of them. Rondo recognized the other men from town, and they nodded somberly at each other.

"Am I glad to see you fellows," Ross broke the silence.

Ross was the sheriff at Empty-lake. He had a tall and lanky frame, with tanned skin and brown hair. When he spoke he always displayed a rich, Texas drawl.

Using his thumb, Ross pushed the brim of his hat up. He took in a big breath, let it out, and looked at Rondo.

"I have bad news," he announced, his voice grim.

"We figured you did," Rondo said.

"It's about Rachel and April."

51

Rondo's face filled with concern while Lee looked startled.

"What about her?" Rondo asked, his voice curt.

"She's been taken," Ross declared, and added, "April too."

"Taken by whom?"

"Injuns."

"This far south?" Rondo looked doubtful. "Injuns haven't raided down here in years."

"Well, these Injuns did," Ross said sourly. "They attacked the Tomlin's headquarters. Rachel and April were out riding, and they never showed back up."

"June?" Lee spoke, his voice hoarse.

"She's fine," Ross reassured. "She was with the Tomlins."

"And the Tomlins?" Rondo asked.

"Mr. Tomlin got a bullet in the shoulder, and Buster got hit in the leg. Other than that, they're fine. They were holed up at the main house and were able to fight 'em off."

Rondo nodded, and his face paled as his thoughts returned to Rachel.

"When did this happen?" Cooper spoke up.

"Two days back."

"Find out anything?"

"Some," Ross nodded. "Tracks are heading northwest. Big bunch too, around thirty horses. We trailed 'em for a day, but then we ran out of supplies."

"Are you going after them?"

Before Ross could reply, Jeremiah Wisdom spoke up.

"I am," he said in a quiet, stern voice.

Jeremiah had a long history with the Landons. An educated man, he was cunning and careful. He was tall and thin, and his face was dark from the sun. He spoke the Apache language fluently and was also a clever poker player.

Jeremiah had been on the wrong side of the law for several years. Recently, he'd been attempting to live an honest life by owning and operating The Palace Hotel.

Everybody was also aware of his feelings for April, including Lee.

Yancy studied Jeremiah with thoughtful eyes and cleared his throat.

"You know about Injuns," he recalled.

"Some," Jeremiah nodded.

"Care to speculate which tribe it was?"

"Direction they're headed, I'd say Apaches. Them, or Kiowas."

"Make any difference?"

"Nope. Neither one likes us."

"I was afraid of that," Yancy said. He glanced at Cooper and added, "Well, there's only one thing to do."

"What's that?" Ross spoke back up.

"Go get 'em back."

Chapter twenty

"What about Lucy Nash?" Rondo looked at Yancy.

"She can wait," he replied.

Rondo looked thoughtful and said, "You and Coop did this before, when you got Wyatt back."

"That's right."

"How exactly did you accomplish that?" Rondo asked. "You never told us."

Yancy glanced at his brother, and Cooper cleared his throat and took over.

"The plan was to trade for Wyatt, but we lost our trading goods," he explained. "We had to find another way."

"And what was that?" Lee asked.

"Well, a thunderstorm helped."

"A thunderstorm?"

Cooper nodded.

"That's nice, but we can't count on a thunderstorm," Lee pointed out with a hint of sarcasm.

"I wouldn't suggest it," Cooper agreed.

"How about trading for Rachel and April?" Rondo asked, and there was hope in his voice. "If we pooled our money together, we could buy some trade goods."

"I don't think so," Jeremiah spoke up, and everybody looked at him.

"Why not?" Rondo demanded.

"This wasn't a normal Injun raid," Jeremiah explained. "They traveled all this way and only attacked one ranch. Seems odd to me."

"Almost sounds personal," Yancy said.

"It does," Jeremiah agreed.

Yancy looked thoughtful, but didn't reply.

"We can figure this out later," Lee broke in impatiently. "We're wasting time. Let's get a move on."

"There's no need for you to come along," Jeremiah shot Lee a dark look.

"Why's that?" Lee narrowed his eyes.

"We don't need your sort."

"What sort would that be?"

"You know."

Rage filled Lee's face, but Yancy spoke before he could reply.

"Hold it. Both of you," his voice was stern. "Lee has just as much right to come along as the rest of us. But, there's a right way and a wrong way to go about this."

A few tense seconds passed. Jeremiah scowled but remained silent while Lee breathed deeply, exhaled, and nodded.

"What do you suggest?" He asked.

Yancy didn't reply. He looked at his brother, and Cooper took over.

"First thing we've got to understand," he said, "is that we ain't gonna catch them unless they *want* us to."

"I'm not sure about that," Lee argued. "I can travel fast. Especially alone."

"The Apaches can travel faster," Cooper replied matter-of-factly. "And, they have a two day lead on us."

Lee frowned, but didn't reply.

"Expect to be gone a while," Cooper continued. "We won't catch 'em until they stop, and that probably won't happen until they're safe in the mountains."

"That could take weeks," Lee objected.

"Sure could," Cooper agreed. "So, first thing, we'll ride to town and gather some supplies."

"Then what?" Lee asked.

"We'll start tracking them."

Lee pinched his face in thought and nodded slowly.

"Sounds like a reasonable plan," he finally said.

Cooper looked at the rest of them.

"Any objections?"

Nobody said anything.

"All right," Cooper said. "Let's get to town."

Everybody mounted up. They kicked up their horses, and Ross fell in beside Yancy.

"I'd like to come along," he offered.

Yancy thought it over and shook his head.

"No, a sheriff belongs in his town."

Ross frowned reluctantly, and no more words were spoken as they trotted towards town.

Chapter twenty-one

Brian had a lot on his mind.

He was deeply concerned about Lee, April, and June, and he was worried about their hotel.

There was also Jeremiah Wisdom to consider. Brian rode beside him, and he looked disturbed and slightly irritated.

This troubled Brian, because he knew a confrontation was building between Jeremiah and Lee concerning April.

"You had a long night," Brian spoke, attempting to start a conversation.

Jeremiah glanced up from his brooding.

"You say something?"

"You rode a long ways last night," Brian tried again.

"I reckon we did."

Brian nodded. It was silent a moment, and he asked, "With you gone, who's running the hotel?"

"My partner."

Brian was startled.

"Partner?"

"That's right."

"I wasn't aware you had another partner."

"I was short on money."

Brian didn't like that, and he frowned his disapproval.

"A hotel is supposed to bring *in* money," he reminded. "When we left, you had over twenty thousand dollars. What happened to it?"

"I had a bad run at poker, just like Lee did."

"How bad?"

"Bad enough."

Brian scowled at that.

"You should have asked Jessica Tussle before you took on another partner," he scolded.

Jeremiah was tiring of the conversation.

"How could I? I haven't even met her."

"That's why Lee and I are here," Brian informed.

"Oh?"

"Jessica isn't your partner anymore. She sold out, so to speak."

"To whom?"

"Me and Lee."

Jeremiah's face remained blank, and he said in a curt voice, "Not sure what to think about that."

"And I'm not sure what to think about your new partner," Brian said.

Jeremiah grunted.

"Right now, all I care about is getting April back," he said.

"Are you two good friends now?" Brian pried for information.

"We're more than that."

"I'm not sure if you're aware, but Lee and April are also close," Brian warned. "*Very* close."

"I'm aware."

A few tense seconds passed, and Brian commented, "Well, there'll be plenty of time to figure things out later."

"Should be."

"There'll be a lot to figure out too."

"Yes," Jeremiah replied. "It would appear so."

Chapter twenty-two

They reached town midmorning.

Empty-lake was mostly a cow town of some two-dozen buildings. Two establishments stood out the most. The sheriff's office built by the late Lieutenant Porter, and The Palace Hotel.

Rondo, Lee, and Brian received curious looks as they walked their horses down the main street. They halted at the general store, dismounted, and tied their horses to the hitching railing.

Yancy, Cooper, and Rondo went inside while Jeremiah hurried over to the hotel. Ross walked across the street to check in at the sheriff's office, and Lee and Brian stayed with the horses.

While they had a moment, Brian told Lee about Jeremiah's new partner. Lee listened, but Brian could tell that he was only partly interested.

"Should we meet this new partner before we head out?" Brian wondered.

"You do what you think best," Lee replied.

"I was asking your opinion."

"Right now, I just don't care."

"But it's *our* hotel," Brian objected.

Lee just grunted his response.

Brian looked thoughtful as he watched Jeremiah come out of the hotel and walk towards them.

"I reckon it can wait," he finally said.

***

They packed their supplies on Jug-head and No-see-ums, and then they untied their horses and mounted up.

Ross stood by and watched them.

"Good luck," he said.

59

"Thanks," Rondo said.

Ross looked wistful while Yancy glanced around at everyone.

"Everybody ready?" He asked.

They nodded, so Yancy kicked up his horse. Cooper followed, and he led Jug-head. Next in line was Rondo, followed by Lee, Brian and No-see-ums, and then Jeremiah.

Chapter twenty-three

They rode west, towards the Tomlin's headquarters. The mood was somber, and nobody talked.

It was a five-mile ride.

As they trotted up, they spotted Mr. Tomlin sitting on the porch beside his wife. His shoulder was bandaged, but he still managed to hold his rifle across his lap.

Buster was also on the porch; his leg bandaged and hiked up on the railing.

Rory and June were in front of the house, on their hands and knees, playing a game of marbles.

The game came to an abrupt halt when they were spotted. June retreated to the porch, and Rory grabbed his rifle and stood by the steps.

Their faces were tense, but everyone relaxed when they recognized the Landons.

They dismounted, tied their horses to the hitching rail, and walked towards the main house.

Lee was slightly behind, and June didn't recognize him until he had reached the porch steps.

A small cry came from her lips, and tears spilled down her face as she ran toward him.

A hesitant smile crossed Lee's face. June hugged him, and Lee was surprised at how fiercely she clung to him.

"Now, now," Lee said gruffly, and he patted her on the back. "What's this?"

"I knew you'd come back! I just knew it!"

Lee didn't know what to say, and he looked uncomfortable.

"I'm here," he finally said.

Jeremiah stood nearby, and he watched the scene with an emotionless face.

Lee finally pulled away, but June held his hand firmly as they joined everybody on the porch.

"We heard what happened," Rondo was saying, and added, "We're going after them."

"If anybody can get them back, it'll be you fellows," Mr. Tomlin declared, and he added bitterly, "It's been difficult, just sitting here, not being able to do anything."

"We'll get Rachel back, and April too," Rondo declared.

"I know you will."

Yancy cleared his throat.

"Do the Apaches have any grudges against you, Mr. Tomlin? Seems odd they would travel all this way just to attack your ranch."

"Seemed strange to me too," Mr. Tomlin agreed. "But, I can't think of anything. 'Course, I've fought Injuns before, but so have a lot of folks."

Yancy nodded thoughtfully, but didn't say anything.

"Well, we'd best be on our way," Rondo spoke up. "We just wanted you to be aware of the situation."

"God go with you," Mr. Tomlin declared as they left the porch.

June walked with Lee to his horse. He tried to release her hand, but she held on firmly.

"I've got to go, June," Lee said softly.

"Don't go," she whimpered. "Not again."

"June," Lee knelt beside her. "I'm going to fetch your Ma. When we get back, the three of us are going to spend some time together. Would you like that?"

June's piercing blue eyes stared straight into Lee's, and he felt a pull on his heartstrings.

"Yes," June said. "I would."

"All right then," Lee said.

He straightened up, stepped into the saddle, and looked down at her.

"I'll be back," he promised.

"I'll be waiting," June swallowed hard and tried to look brave.

Lee nodded, and no more words were spoken as they rode out.

Chapter twenty-four

Jeremiah took the lead, and he rode to the spot where the Indians had set up camp.

By then it was late in the day. They tended to their horses, built a fire, cooked supper, and made coffee.

"Tracks have faded now, but yesterday I found some women's tracks over there," Jeremiah gestured. "Strides were normal too."

"That's good," Rondo looked hopeful.

"Two women?" Lee spoke up.

"At least."

"You think there were more?" Lee raised an eyebrow.

"Can't say. It's possible. Tracks were real mingled."

Lee pinched his face in thought.

"Well, at least they made it this far," he said.

"How much further did you follow the tracks?" Yancy spoke up.

"Four, five miles."

"See anymore sign of the women?"

"No."

Yancy frowned at that, but didn't say anything.

It was silent then, and everybody sat there thinking their own thoughts. After supper, Yancy got everyone set on the night watch, and they turned in.

Jeremiah had the first watch, and he sat by the campfire and watched as Lee rolled out his bedroll. Nobody else was near, so Jeremiah lowered his voice.

"You made a lot of promises to June back there," he said, his voice curt.

Lee narrowed his eyes.

"I meant every one."

"You already hurt her once," Jeremiah said. "I'd hate to see it happen again."

"It won't."

"You might as well know," Jeremiah said. "April and I have discussed marriage. More than once."

"Did she say yes?"

"Well, no, not yet," Jeremiah looked slightly flustered. "But she will. Understand?"

"Completely," Lee smiled tightly. He crawled into his bedroll and added, "Night."

Jeremiah watched him a moment before he spoke.

"Sure," he replied.

Chapter twenty-five

Night settled over the camp.

Brian was the first to fall asleep, and everybody else tossed and turned while they listened to his steady snoring.

Cooper and Yancy were on the other side of camp, and Yancy sighed.

"I thought you said we wouldn't have to listen to that tonight," he commented.

"Guess I was wrong," Cooper replied.

Yancy grunted softly, and it was silent for a few moments.

"Something doesn't feel right about this," Yancy suddenly said.

"I know what you mean."

"I can't figure why those Injuns would travel all this way, just to attack one ranch."

"And then give up so easily," Cooper added.

"Makes you wonder if they want us to follow."

"It does, don't it."

"We've got to be careful," Yancy warned. "An ambush is likely."

"I'd say it's a strong possibility," Cooper agreed. "Especially once we're close to the mountains."

"And another thing," Yancy continued. "Besides Brian, you and I are the only ones not emotionally involved. We've got to keep our wits about us, and set a good example."

"Rondo and Lee will be fine," Cooper reassured. "They've been in tough situations before."

"But this concerns their women folk," Yancy reminded. "That could cloud their judgment."

Cooper frowned at that.

"I reckon it could," he admitted.

"Just something to keep in mind."

Before Cooper could reply, Brian snorted in his sleep. He made some strange moaning sounds, and then he returned to his snoring routine.

Yancy scowled and then sighed.

"Well, we'd best get some sleep," he suggested, and he rolled over and pulled his blankets up around him.

"Good luck with that," Cooper replied.

Chapter twenty-six

Not much happened during the next three days.

Rondo and Cooper were the best trackers, so they took the lead. Everyone else followed, and they kept their eyes on the surrounding landscape, looking for anything suspicious.

The terrain changed as they rode west. There were fewer trees about, and the gentle hills flattened out. There also wasn't as much grass.

Nobody talked much, and the mood was somber. Brian could feel the tension between Lee and Jeremiah, and he purposely rode between them as much as possible.

At the end of the first day, they rode up to a small creek.

There were some tracks leading away from the main group, and Yancy and Cooper followed them. They found five graves, and there were Indians in all five.

They rode by several dead horses on the second day. They didn't lose ground, but they didn't gain any either.

They arrived at a dirt tank towards the end of the third day. The tank was filled with rainwater, and there was also the remains of a small fire, plus the carcass of a dead horse.

"Hold up!" Cooper held up his hand.

"What is it?" Jeremiah asked as everybody halted.

"Lots of tracks scattered about," Cooper explained as he and Rondo dismounted. "I don't want to wipe anything out."

Jeremiah nodded, and several minutes passed while Rondo and Cooper walked in a big circle. Finally, they came together and knelt close to the tank.

"What is it?" Jeremiah asked, his voice impatient.

"A few of them went this way," Cooper gestured, and he glanced at Jeremiah. "What do you think?"

"Mebbe another Apache died," he suggested.

"Could be," Cooper agreed, and he looked at Yancy. "I reckon we should find out."

"I'll go," Rondo offered, and Lee nodded.

"No," Yancy's voice was surprisingly firm. "Coop and I will take a look."

Nobody objected, and Yancy glanced at the sun.

"Be dark soon," he said. "Might as well make camp here."

Everyone agreed, and Yancy and Cooper rode out.

Chapter twenty-seven

"Any sign of the women?" Lee asked as they unsaddled their horses.

"Nothing for sure. Tracks are too mingled," Rondo replied.

"I was afraid of that," Lee frowned.

Once the horses were tended to, Jeremiah offered to gather some firewood. Brian went with him, and Rondo and Lee set up camp.

Lee leaned against his saddle after they had finished. He pulled out a cigar, bit off the end, struck a match on his saddle horn, lit the cigar, and took a deep puff.

His face looked thoughtful as he exhaled.

"Been thinking," he said.

"Oh?" Rondo raised an eyebrow.

"You have Rachel, Cooper has Josie, and Yancy has Jessica."

"If she's still alive," Rondo said, his face dark.

"We can't think that way," Lee frowned at his friend. "Rachel's alive, and so is April."

A wistful look crossed Rondo's face.

"She'd better be."

"Josie lived with the Apaches," Lee reminded. "She told me once they never kill women or kids unless they have good reason."

"Josie would know."

"She sure would."

Rondo nodded, and it was silent for a bit.

"If we get through this, I'm gonna ask for April's hand in marriage," Lee suddenly said. "She might say no, but I'm still going to ask."

Rondo studied Lee with a thoughtful look.

"It's about time," he said.

"She's a good woman," Lee continued. "And, June's a good kid."

"I'd say so."

"We'd get along just fine. And, now that I'm back in the hotel business, I'd have something to offer."

"I don't think she cares about that. She just wants you."

Before Lee could reply, they heard the sound of a horse.

"Here they come," Rondo said, and they stood.

Jeremiah and Brian walked in with armfuls of firewood, and Yancy trotted up behind them. His face was grim.

"Where's Cooper?" Rondo asked, confused.

"He'll be along."

Rondo nodded and asked, "Find anything?"

Yancy nodded somberly.

"Back in the rocks," he said softly. "We found another body."

"An Injun?" Lee spoke up.

"No, it was a woman," Yancy replied. He paused and added, "A white woman."

Nobody spoke, and the silence was heavy.

"Was it Rachel?" Rondo finally asked, his voice husky.

"Couldn't tell," Yancy said. "We don't know who it was."

"What do you mean?" Lee demanded.

Yancy sighed, gathered his thoughts, and continued.

"She was scalped, and her body was all cut up and swollen. From the looks of it, she's been dead a day or two. Cooper stayed to give her a decent burial."

"You mean those Apaches didn't even bother to bury her?" Brian asked.

Yancy nodded curtly.

"I'm going back," Lee demanded. "I can recognize her."

"Me too," Rondo and Jeremiah declared.

They started toward their horses, but Yancy stopped them.

"No," he said, and his voice was hard. "It wouldn't do any of you any good. I tell you she's unrecognizable. Don't ask me to explain it anymore than that."

"But we've got to know who it is," Rondo objected, and his voice almost broke.

"We catch those Apaches, and we'll know."

Several tense seconds passed as everybody thought on that, and Rondo nodded sullenly.

"All right," he vowed. "We'll catch them, if it's the last thing I ever do. And then, they'll be sorry."

Lee and Jeremiah nodded their agreement, and no more words were spoken.

Part Three
"Winchester, Apache Scout"

Chapter twenty-eight

As the days flew by, time blended together for Rachel. She had no idea what day it was, or exactly how long they'd been captives.

The days became repetitive. Each morning they rode out before daylight, and they kept up the grueling pace until dark.

It was a demanding routine, but it only took Rachel and April a few days to adapt. They didn't talk much, or cause trouble.

Water was scarce, and every few days a horse would collapse. When this happened, the Apaches would usually stop, make camp, and eat.

By now, Rachel didn't mind the taste of horsemeat so much.

They finally slowed their pace as they neared the New Mexico Mountains. There was a pass looming in front of them, and they were heading towards it.

The Indians' moods had lifted. They laughed and called out to each other often, and they seemed to be less on guard.

They were about a day's ride from the foothills when No Worries stopped in the middle of the day. Rachel was surprised, because no horse had collapsed.

They set up camp on top of a steep, little hill that was well covered in brush. There was also a dirt tank filled with water, fed by an underground spring.

Rachel and April were allowed to drink their fill. Afterwards they were escorted off to the side of camp, and nobody paid them much attention.

"Why'd we stop?" April spoke, her voice low.

"Don't know, but I'm not complaining," Rachel replied as she stretched. "Maybe this is the last water hole for a few days."

It fell silent then, and Rachel wrinkled her brow in thought as she watched the Indians.

With No Worries supervising, they dragged up some brush and dug trenches in several spots. To Rachel, it seemed they were preparing to keep watch behind them.

April was thinking the same thing.

"Do you think somebody's trailing us?" She asked.

"Perhaps," Rachel replied.

"Lee and Rondo?"

"Could be."

"The Apaches are setting up an ambush," April said, and there was worry in her voice.

"That, or a few of them are staying here to keep watch," Rachel reasoned. "If I were them, I'd wait to ambush whoever's following until we reach the pass. It's too open around here."

"Makes sense," April agreed. She hesitated, and asked, "Do you still think Lee and Rondo are coming for us?"

"Of course."

"But so much time has passed."

"I'm sure they had to get organized," Rachel replied. "It could be several weeks before they show up."

"By that time, we might be Indian wives," April objected.

"That, or we'll be slaves."

April scowled, and then she gave Rachel a concerned look as another thought occurred to her.

"How are you?" She asked, and added quietly, "With the baby, I mean."

"I'm not sure," Rachel looked worried. "I think everything's fine. I don't feel any pain anywhere."

"That's a good thing," April replied. A few seconds passed, and she chuckled wryly.

"What is it?" Rachel asked, anxious for a light moment.

"If they make wives out of us, your Indian husband is sure going to be surprised in nine months."

Rachel shuddered at the thought.

"If we're given the opportunity to choose, I'd rather be a slave," April added.

"I'd rather be neither," Rachel said.

Chapter twenty-nine

Unaware to the Apaches, a white man was nearby, watching with great interest.

A harsh dryness had settled in his throat. The hot, afternoon sun was unmerciful, and the desert sand he lay on burned his lean, hard body.

He was nestled down between two shrubs, and he was nearly invisible.

Sweat trickled down his whisker-stubbled jaw, but he paid it no mind. His teeth ground slowly as he chewed a mouthful of tobacco, and he spit out a long, brown stream, aimed at a nearby chuckwalla lizard. Other than that, he didn't move a muscle.

He grunted wolfishly as the chuckwalla flicked its tongue distastefully at him and scampered away.

He had on a worn, sweat-soaked buckskin shirt, and the faded army pants he wore blended perfectly with the desert terrain.

Knee-high moccasins were on his feet. An army knife was thrust inside his left moccasin for easy access, and a battered hat was crumpled underneath him. Beside him was a Winchester '73, and on his hip he displayed a Colt six-shooter.

August Landon, known as Winchester, was in his late twenties. He was currently an Apache scout for the army.

A very handsome man, he had a boyish smile, long, sandy brown hair, and light eyes. Standing at nearly six feet, he was thin but also muscular.

He squinted his eyes against the sun as he studied the countryside.

In front of him was a hill covered with brush, and he could smell campfire smoke. Behind him, many miles away, were the New Mexico Mountains.

That was the direction he had come from. He was on his way south, to report his findings to the nearest army post.

His orders had been clear-cut. Find No Worries' summer camp, and report back immediately. Simple as that sounded, the task had turned out to be difficult.

After weeks of scouting and cutting trails, he had finally found their camp. However, No Worries and his warriors weren't there. All he'd seen were women, children, and older braves.

This had weighed heavily on Winchester's mind as he made his way down the mountains. He took great measures to cover his tracks, and he was relieved when he finally reached the foothills.

But then, his exhausted horse took a fatal misstep and broke his leg. Not wanting to risk the sound of a shot, Winchester had regretfully cut the horse's throat.

The nearest army outpost was at least sixty miles, with a lot of rough country between. That was a long walk, but he had no choice.

His main concern was water. His canteen was nearly empty, so he headed for the spring-filled tank at the hill.

With his Winchester in hand, he had traveled in a relentless trot. His eyes had moved constantly as he surveyed the landscape for anything suspicious.

As he'd neared the tank, his nostrils caught the slight hint of mesquite smoke, and he dropped flat.

It then took him thirty minutes to work his way around to where he was now. He still didn't see any Apaches, but he knew they were there.

He needed to know if it was No Worries' bunch, but he was in no hurry. He was in a good spot, and he would wait for the Apaches to make a move.

An hour later, the Apaches finally showed. They were horseback, and they were riding straight towards him.

Chapter thirty

Winchester sucked in his breath, and he flattened himself against the ground as much as possible.

A muscled, proud looking Apache rode in front. He was the tallest Indian Winchester had ever seen, and he'd seen a lot the past few years.

Winchester knew without a doubt that this warrior was No Worries. Even the way he sat on his horse displayed leadership.

His eyes went down the line. He counted eighteen Apaches, plus two captive women.

His curiosity grew as he studied the women. They were both young and looked sturdy. Even from afar, he could see their undeniable strength in their faces.

He felt a pinch of sympathy, but there was nothing he could do. The best way he could help was to reach that army post as fast as possible.

He avoided eye contact as the Apaches drew closer.

He didn't know if it was true or not, but he'd heard that Indians could tell when the enemy was watching them, and he didn't want to take that chance.

They were riding straight towards him, and sweat poured from his brow. Moving his hand slowly, he gripped his rifle in anticipation.

With his finger on the trigger, he watched No Worries' face. Any second now he expected to be spotted. If he had to die, he was determined to take No Worries with him.

But then, No Worries turned his horse to the side. He was following an old trail, and he was only twenty yards or so from Winchester as he passed by.

Winchester didn't even breathe. They were so close he could smell them, and he suddenly realized that he needed to spit out a stream of tobacco.

Unexpectedly, an Apache warrior jumped from his horse. He was shirtless, and his stout, built muscles rippled as he ran in the direction of Winchester. His eyes glowed with triumph, and he held a wooden club, ready to strike.

A surge of fear passed through Winchester, but he remained still. He pulled the hammer back on his rifle and waited.

The Apache stopped abruptly only a short distance from him. He swung his club, and Winchester heard a loud thump, followed by a grunt of satisfaction.

Winchester blinked as the Apache bent over. When he straightened up, Winchester spotted the chuckwalla lizard in his hand.

The Apache uttered a chilling, high-pitched war cry, and then he sprinted back to his horse.

Winchester was startled, but he somehow managed to stay still. Seconds later, he realized that he had swallowed his tobacco. He felt the strong urge to cough, but he forced himself not to.

The band of Apaches grew smaller as they traveled on. They were heading towards the mountains, and they finally became blurs and then disappeared in the distance.

Only then did Winchester move. He rose to one knee, put on his hat, and took a careful look around.

He saw or heard nothing, so he stood and headed for the tank. He yearned for a cool drink of water to quench his nagging thirst.

He covered ground quickly with his long strides. The tank was just ahead, and he could almost smell the water.

Winchester heard a faint noise, and he dropped flat. He scarcely breathed as he listened, but he didn't hear anything else.

He raised his head and looked around. He saw nothing, so he crawled over to some rocks. He took a peek between them, and he spotted three Indian ponies. They were beside the tank, tied to some trees.

Beyond the tank, at the top of the hill, were three Apaches. They had dug in, and their backs were to him as they watched their back trail intently.

Winchester took in a big breath and sighed silently.

Chapter thirty-one

Winchester didn't move for a long time, and neither did the Apaches.

His mind worked furiously as he thought on the situation.

He finally came to the conclusion that someone must be following the Apaches. He figured these Apaches had been left to keep watch, and to give No Worries fair warning when they were spotted.

In a way, this pleased Winchester. All he had to do now was follow the tracks until he ran into whoever was following the Apaches. Hopefully, he could borrow a horse and continue on to the army outpost.

Winchester gave a long, lustful look at the tank of water. He was tempted to crawl over and fill his canteen, but he quickly dismissed this idea.

If spotted, he might be able to take on one or even two Apaches, but not three.

Being as quiet as possible, he slid backwards until he could no longer see the Apaches or the tank. Then he waited, listening for any sound.

He heard nothing, and Winchester grunted softly in satisfaction. He rose to one knee and uncapped his canteen.

He took two, long swallows. The water was lukewarm, but it tasted mighty good. He swished it around his mouth some before swallowing, and he sighed wistfully as he recapped his empty canteen.

"It'll have to do," he said softly.

Winchester rose to his full height. He took a slow, careful look around, and then he moved out in his relentless trot.

He took no chances. He circled out at least half a mile, and then he made his way back to the tracks.

They were easy to follow, and his moccasins hardly made any sound at all with his long, reaching strides.

For some reason, Winchester felt a great urgency to reach whoever was following the Apaches. He sensed that something important was about to happen, and he quickened his pace.

Part Four
"Strained Family Reunion"

Chapter thirty-two

The days flew by, and their routine never changed. Before they knew it, nearly three weeks had passed.

They were now deep in the New Mexico Territory. They could see the mountains, and they looked hazy and dark blue.

Since finding the dead woman, everyone's moods had darkened even more. But, nobody discussed it. Instead, they just focused on the task at hand.

Rondo, Lee, and Jeremiah hardly talked at all, and Lee and Jeremiah wouldn't even look at each other. Everybody could feel the tension building between them.

On this particular day, Jeremiah rode beside Yancy. His face was heavy and mulish.

From time to time, Yancy glanced sideways at him. Finally, he cleared his throat.

"You all right?"

"Sure. Why do you ask?" Jeremiah replied abruptly.

"Only because of the miserable look on your face."

Jeremiah looked away and sighed.

"Is it obvious?"

"Is to me," Yancy said. A few seconds passed, and he asked, "What's on your mind?"

"You really want to know?"

"Wouldn't have asked if I didn't."

Jeremiah hesitated, but then explained, "This is all my fault."

"How's that?" Yancy raised an eyebrow.

"If I hadn't been pressing so hard for April's hand in marriage, she would have been with me when the attack happened. And, if she had been with me, she and Rachel wouldn't have been out riding."

"There's a lot of 'ifs' in there," Yancy objected.

"And now, she could be dead," Jeremiah declared.

"We don't know that."

"But it's possible."

"Anything is," Yancy tried again.

"I keep praying April is alive. But that makes me feel guilty, because if she *is* alive, that means Rachel's not."

"You're being mighty hard on yourself."

"Do you want to know what really irritates me?" Jeremiah continued as he ignored Yancy's comment.

"Might as well."

"She doesn't even love me. She loves *him*," Jeremiah nodded ahead at Lee. "I changed my ways. Been living right, doing things honest, and she never even noticed."

"I hate to admit it, but so has Lee."

Jeremiah grunted at that, and several seconds passed.

"Is April the reason you changed?" Yancy finally asked.

Jeremiah thought a moment.

"Mostly."

"Then you're looking at it all wrong."

"How's that?" Jeremiah shot Yancy a dark look.

"Change because *you* want to. Do it for yourself, and you'll notice."

"What about April?"

"If she hasn't noticed, then she might not be the one for you," Yancy said bluntly. "That's something you'll have to deal with."

"And if I can't?"

"April isn't the only woman out there. You keep doing things honest, stay out of trouble, and the right woman will come along and take notice."

Jeremiah pinched his face in thought.

"What if no other woman will do?"

"Then you and Lee might have a problem," Yancy replied.

Jeremiah frowned, and it was silent for a bit.

"What you say makes sense, somewhat," he finally admitted.

"Thanks," Yancy said wryly.

"Must be a moral in there someplace. I'll think on it."

"You do that," Yancy said.

Chapter thirty-three

They made camp that night in amongst a small cluster of trees. After supper, they sat around the campfire. Nobody talked as they thought their own thoughts.

By now, even Yancy was tiring of the silence. He glanced at Cooper and cleared his throat.

"Are we closing the gap any?"

"Not much," Cooper shook his head. "We're three, four days behind. Mebbe more."

"So, we ain't gonna catch them until we reach the mountains," Lee spoke up, stating the obvious.

"Unless we ride into an ambush," Cooper warned.

"What if they split up? What'll we do then?" Lee wanted to know.

"Yancy and I know where their summer camp is," Cooper replied. "They'll probably go there."

"Then what?"

"Then we'll see," Yancy said.

"How big is this camp?" Rondo entered the conversation.

"Biggest one I've ever seen," Yancy replied.

"Long and narrow?"

"Sorta," Yancy nodded. "It's spread out beside a river, down in a valley."

Rondo looked thoughtful.

"A diversion of some sort might work," he suggested.

"Perhaps," Yancy said.

Suddenly, Cooper tilted his head. He made a motion to be quiet, and several seconds passed.

"What is it?" Jeremiah hissed.

"I heard something," Cooper replied, and he glanced at Yancy. "Somebody's out there."

Yancy didn't question it. If Cooper hadn't been sure, he wouldn't have said anything.

"Spread out," Yancy hissed.

Everybody drew their Colts and backed into the darkness.

A long minute passed, and everybody listened hard.

"Hello the camp!" A hoarse voice suddenly called out, and everyone was surprised at how close he was.

"Who's out there?" Yancy demanded.

"Just a weary stranger."

"Come on in," Yancy said. "But move slow."

Out of the dark, a lone man came walking in. He was tall and rawboned, his jaw square and his mouth firm. In one hand he carried a Winchester, but he held it low, being careful not to show any hostility.

Yancy frowned as he studied him. He was vaguely familiar, but Yancy couldn't place him.

"Lose your horse?" Yancy asked.

"Some miles back," he said.

His eyes went over everyone in camp, and then he looked back at Yancy.

"I'm Winchester, Apache scout."

"Heard of you," Yancy said, and there was disapproval in his voice.

Winchester had quite the reputation.

He was known all across the New Mexico Territory and Arizona Territory. He had killed several men in gunfights, and his eagerness to kill was feared by many.

He had become an Apache scout for the army to avoid jail time. As a scout, he had quickly gained a reputation for his recklessness and roughness.

"I'm a mite thirsty," Winchester said. "It's been a while since my last swig."

Cooper tossed him a canteen, and he drank like a man who had been lost in the desert for days without water.

He sighed wistfully as he lowered the canteen. He coughed and wiped his mouth with his sleeve.

"'Preciate it," he said, and he offered the canteen back to Cooper.

"Keep it."

"Thanks. I will."

"Hungry?" Cooper asked.

"I could eat."

"Got some coffee and salt pork," Cooper gestured at the fire.

Winchester nodded his head in acceptance, so Cooper filled a plate, poured some coffee, and handed it to him.

He sat cross-legged by the fire and wolfed it down.

Everybody had questions, but nobody spoke. Instead, they waited patiently.

Several minutes passed, and Winchester heaved a sigh of satisfaction. He placed his empty plate to the side, refilled his coffee cup, and glanced up at everyone.

"That tasted mighty good," he said.

"Glad you liked it," Cooper replied.

Yancy had been watching him with his face pinched in thought. Suddenly, he grunted in surprise.

"You're not Winchester," he accused.

"I beg your pardon?" He stood and shot Yancy a dark look.

"You're August Landon."

Surprise showed in his eyes.

"How'd you figure that?"

"Because I'm Yancy Landon."

"Well, I'll be," Winchester said, surprised. "How 'bout that."

Several seconds passed as everybody thought on that, and Lee cleared his throat and looked at Yancy.

"Let me get this straight," Lee said. "Winchester is *your* cousin?"

"Looks like," Yancy said, and he scowled at the thought.

Despite his foul mood, Lee almost smiled.

Chapter thirty-four

"I thought you looked sorta familiar," Winchester told Yancy. "You've changed since the war."

"So have you," Yancy replied.

Winchester smiled at that.

"I reckon we all have," he said, and then he turned to Cooper. "You must be Cooper."

"That's right," Cooper said, and they shook hands.

"Who's this?" Winchester turned to Rondo.

"I'm Rondo Landon."

"I figured you was," Winchester looked pleased. "I've heard about that ivory handled Colt. We almost met once."

"We did?" Rondo looked interested.

Winchester didn't explain as he turned to Lee, and it was silent while they studied each other.

"You have the look of a Landon too," Winchester finally said. "But, I can't place you."

"Landon? Me?" Lee snorted. "I'm not a Landon. My name's Lee Mattingly."

Winchester whistled his admiration.

"I've heard of you. You have quite the reputation."

"So do you," Lee replied.

"I get around," Winchester grinned.

Next, Cooper introduced Jeremiah and Brian, and they nodded at each other.

"August," Yancy spoke back up. "What are you doing out here?"

"My name is Winchester," he corrected gruffly.

"That's not the name your parents gave you."

"I despise my real name," he retorted. "I wasn't even born in August."

They frowned at each other, and several seconds passed.

"You were always coming up with nicknames when we were younger," Yancy recalled.

"That's right."

"I figured you might have grown up by now," Yancy said.

Winchester narrowed his eyes and thrust out his jaw.

"What do you mean by that remark?"

"Just that."

"And *you* always had a bad habit of speaking your mind," Winchester accused.

Before Yancy could reply, Cooper jumped in and changed the subject.

"How'd you come up with Winchester?" He asked.

Winchester stared at Yancy for a moment more, and then he glanced at Cooper.

"I had to cover a feller with my rifle a while back," he explained. "The feller said, 'Hey Winchester, watch where you're pointing that thing', and it sorta stuck."

"How's your brother, Quincy?" Cooper asked.

"Haven't seen him."

"Oh? Is he alive?" Cooper looked concerned.

"Last I heard he was."

Cooper nodded, relieved.

"Just how many Landons are there?" Lee entered the conversation, and he looked confused.

"Just Quincy," Cooper explained. "You see, our Pa had two brothers named Walt and Noley. Walt was the oldest, and Noley was nine years younger. You remember him."

"Rondo's Pa," Lee nodded. "He was a good man."

"Walt had three sons," Cooper continued. "Quincy is the oldest, and August is the youngest."

"*Winchester*," Winchester corrected, irritation in his voice.

"What happened to the middle son?" Lee asked.

"He got washed away in a flood when we were youngsters," Cooper explained.

Lee was obviously startled.

"Washed away?"

"Yep, and they never found him," Cooper said, and then he continued. "Anyhow, Quincy is a bit older than me. Then it's me, Yancy, August, and Rondo."

"*Winchester*," he corrected again.

"Yes, *Winchester*," Cooper looked at him and frowned.

Lee looked thoughtful. It looked like he wanted to say something, but he chose not to.

"So, *Winchester*," Yancy spoke up, emphasizing his name. "How'd you lose your horse?"

"It's a long story," Winchester replied, and asked, "Anybody got a chaw of tobacco?"

They all shook their heads.

"I'm a cigar man," Lee explained.

"Nasty habit," Winchester scolded.

"And chewing tobacco ain't?"

They scowled at each other for several seconds.

"I'm not sure I like you," Winchester finally said.

Lee glanced at Jeremiah and looked back at him.

"Get in line," he said sourly.

Chapter thirty-five

Speaking abruptly, Winchester told them about his scouting trip in the mountains. Next, he grabbed a stick and squatted on his heels.

Everybody gathered around him as he traced out a crude map.

"Here are the mountains," he made a small *x* in the dirt. "And we're here, about two days out. And here-," he made another small *x* between them and the mountains, "-is a steep, brushy hill. There's water there, but there's also three Apaches dug in at the top, keeping watch."

Yancy looked thoughtful as he studied the rough drawn map.

"What are they watching for?" He asked.

"You, I reckon."

"Only three?"

"The rest of them rode towards a pass in the mountains," Winchester explained. "My guess is as soon as you're spotted, those Injuns will hightail it to No Worries. They'll be waiting for you in that pass."

"No Worries?" Yancy was startled.

"He was leading them."

Yancy glanced at Cooper and looked back at Winchester.

"We've had dealings with him before," he announced.

"He's a mean Injun," Winchester said, and Cooper nodded his agreement.

"Did you get a good look at them?" Yancy asked.

"I did. Almost too good."

"How many Injuns?"

"Altogether, twenty-one," Winchester replied, and added, "There were also two captive women."

Rondo, Lee, and Jeremiah jumped in surprise.

"Did you say two?" Rondo demanded.

"Sure."

"What did they look like?" Lee asked, his voice anxious.

Winchester thought a moment.

"Well, they were both young, and one had dark hair."

"That sounds like Rachel!" Rondo said, rising excitement in his voice.

"And the other one?" Jeremiah spoke up.

"Her hair was sorta grayish. She might have been a bit older."

Lee and Jeremiah glanced at each other.

"Has to be April," Lee said softly, and Jeremiah nodded his agreement.

Just to know they were alive was a huge relief, and Rondo, Lee, and Jeremiah smiled for the first time in weeks.

Winchester rose to his feet.

"Now, if I could borrow a horse, I'll head for the nearest army post and let them know what's happened," he said.

"You won't help us?" Yancy scowled at him.

"Best way I can is to reach that army post," Winchester replied. "The Army is planning a campaign late this summer."

"We can't wait that long," Yancy replied.

"Why not?"

"The dark headed woman you saw," Rondo spoke up. "She's my wife."

"And the other lady is April," Cooper added. He glanced at Lee and Jeremiah, and said, "She's special too."

Winchester looked at Rondo, and several seconds passed as he thought on it.

"Your wife," he finally said.

"That's right."

"I didn't know that."

"There's no way you could have," Rondo said.

Winchester took in a deep breath and let it out slowly.

"My Pa told me in times of trouble, us Landons have always stuck together," Winchester declared, and added, "I'm already several weeks late. A few more days won't matter."

"So you'll stay?" Rondo asked.

"I'll stay."

"I appreciate that," Rondo said earnestly.

"Don't mention it," Winchester said, and asked, "So, what's the plan?"

Rondo looked around at everyone and said, "We don't have one."

Winchester frowned at that.

"Well, we'd best come up with one," he suggested.

Chapter thirty-six

"Only one thing to do," Winchester declared a few minutes later.

"And what's that?" Yancy looked skeptical.

"They know you're coming," Winchester pointed out. "But, they don't know *when*."

"That sounds about right."

Winchester squatted on his heels and gestured at the map.

"That pass they're headed for is here," he made another small *x* in the dirt. "I just came down that way, and that pass goes all the way up into the mountains. Near the bottom it's narrow, high walled, and mostly rock."

"You think they plan to ambush us there," Yancy said.

"It's a likely spot," Winchester agreed, and added, "That's why we should ambush *them* there."

Everybody was startled.

"How would we do that?" Yancy asked.

"There's an underground spring that bubbles up about a mile up the pass," Winchester explained. "I figure No Worries will wait there."

"Sounds likely," Yancy nodded.

"I say we circle the Injuns at the hill, and ride to the outside of the pass," he traced a small line in the dirt, mapping the route. "It's too steep for a horse, but we could climb those walls on foot. They won't be expecting us, and we could jump 'em from the backside at nighttime. With a little luck, we might even be able to get the women out."

Nobody said anything as they thought on that, and Yancy finally cleared his throat.

"Sounds doable," he said.

"Glad you like it," Winchester said with a hint of strategic pride.

"How about our escape?" Lee wanted to know. "After we ambush them, we'd have to climb that wall again to get back to our horses. Those Injuns would be all over us, even in the dark."

"I didn't say it was a perfect plan," Winchester said defensively.

"Just how narrow is this pass?" Rondo spoke up.

"Narrow," Winchester replied.

"Could two men with rifles hold it?"

Winchester grunted.

"*One* good man could hold off an army," he declared.

Rondo nodded and suggested, "While two of us are holding them off, the rest could go up the pass a ways and climb the wall. Then, whoever's on top could cover the two below while they're catching up."

Yancy nodded slowly.

"Yes, that might work," he said.

"One other thing," Winchester spoke back up. "Even if we manage to pull this off, they'll still be coming after us. And hard."

Everyone nodded their agreement.

"It'll be impossible to outrun them," Winchester pointed out. "Sooner or later they'll catch us, and we'll have us a big fight."

Again, everybody nodded.

"Best place to make a stand would be at the brushy hill," Winchester continued. "There's water there, and plenty of cover. I think we could hold 'em off."

"How long?" Cooper asked.

"Long as we have bullets."

"We brought plenty," Lee said.

"That's a good thing," Winchester smiled. "It's a proven fact. Whoever's best armed usually wins."

"What about the Apaches at the hill?" Jeremiah changed the subject.

"Somebody will have to stay and take care of them," Winchester said matter-of-factly. "Then, they can provide cover fire as we're riding in, just in case we're in trouble."

Everybody glanced at each other, and it was silent while they thought the plan over.

"I say it's worth a try," Yancy finally said. "Anybody object to the idea?"

One by one, everybody shook their heads.

"All right," Yancy declared, and added, "Now, who stays and who goes?"

"I know the way to the pass," Winchester pointed out.

"Rachel's there, so I'm going," Rondo declared.

"I go where April is," Lee said firmly.

"So do I," Jeremiah spoke up.

"And I go with Lee," Brian added.

Yancy studied them a moment, but their determined looks never wavered.

"That leaves me and Coop," he finally said, and everyone nodded.

"That all right with you?" Yancy looked at his older brother.

"I'll do whatever's needed," Cooper replied.

Yancy frowned. He didn't like it, but he finally nodded his agreement.

"It's settled then," he said.

Winchester straightened up and took charge.

"If we leave now, we can reach that pass by tomorrow night," he said. "But, we'll have to ride through the night and all day tomorrow. We won't have time to stop and eat, or get any sleep."

"I haven't slept since this started," Lee grunted. "Let's go."

"I'll need a horse," Winchester said.

Everybody looked at each other, and Cooper spoke up.

"You can ride Jug-head," he offered.

Winchester nodded and asked, "Which one is he?"

Cooper pointed to where Jug-head and No-see-ums were picketed.

"You call that fine looking horse Jug-head?" Winchester frowned his disapproval.

"No. Jug-head is the mule beside him," Cooper corrected.

"What's wrong with the horse?" Winchester scowled.

"He's nearly blind," Lee explained.

Winchester's scowl deepened as he studied the mule.

"I'm not so sure about this," he objected. "We've got to move fast. Perhaps Yancy and I should trade mounts."

"Perhaps not," Yancy declared, his voice firm.

They glared at each other, and Cooper cleared his throat.

"Don't worry," he said. "Jug-head is very, ah, agile."

Winchester didn't look convinced.

"Is he broke to ride?"

"Sometimes," Cooper said with an emotionless face.

"What do you mean by that?" Winchester stared at him.

"Just that."

Chapter thirty-seven

Cooper unpacked Jug-head's pack, and they crammed everything that would fit into No-see-ums' pack. What wouldn't fit, they stuffed in their saddlebags.

Cooper covered Jug-head's back with a blanket and handed the reins to Winchester.

"Can you ride bareback?" Cooper asked.

"Only when I have to," Winchester replied.

"Well, good luck."

"What for?" Winchester looked suspicious.

"Oh, nothing."

Winchester didn't look convinced as he led Jug-head in a circle to loosen him up. Everyone held their breath as he jumped up onto his back.

To everybody's surprise, Jug-head handled perfectly. Winchester trotted him in a circle, spun him around, and made him back up a few feet.

"Say," Winchester said, surprised. "This mule is all right. Travels good, and has a decent handle."

"Glad you like him," Cooper said as he frowned in confusion.

"What's not to like? This mule is smoother than some horses I've ridden."

"You might as well know," Cooper said. "He gets a little cold backed sometimes."

Winchester didn't look convinced.

"Aw, this mule couldn't buck a flea off."

"I'll remember you said that," Yancy spoke up.

"Well, we'd best be going," Winchester changed the subject.

"You fellows go ahead," Cooper offered. "We'll pack up camp."

Rondo, Lee, Brian, and Jeremiah saddled their horses and mounted up.

"We'll see you in a few days," Rondo looked down at Yancy and Cooper.

"Be careful," Yancy replied, his voice soft. "All of you."

"Will do," Rondo replied.

Yancy nodded and glanced at Winchester.

"Don't take any chances," he warned.

"Might not have a choice," Winchester grinned, and he kicked up Jug-head before Yancy could reply.

Rondo, Jeremiah, and Brian fell in behind him, but Lee held back.

Yancy looked troubled.

"Watch him, Lee," he warned.

"What for?" Lee looked interested.

"I don't trust him."

Lee smiled at that.

"When have I heard that before?" He asked, and he kicked up his horse. "Take care," he called over his shoulder.

Yancy didn't reply as he and Cooper watched them disappear into the darkness.

Part Five
"Split Forces"

Chapter thirty-eight

After discussing it, Yancy and Cooper decided to wait until morning to ride out. They had more time than the others, and it would be easier to spot the hill in the daylight.

Cooper made another pot of coffee, and they filled their cups and got comfortable around the fire.

Yancy was silent. He looked troubled, and Cooper glanced at him.

"You don't like this, do you," Cooper said.

"What's that?"

"Staying behind."

"I don't," Yancy admitted.

"Normally I'd agree, but I don't mind so much this time."

"How come?"

"I get shot every time I'm near those mountains," Cooper reminded.

Yancy sighed and shook his head. A few moments passed, and Cooper chuckled.

"At least we don't have to listen to Brian snore tonight," he pointed out.

Yancy grunted at that. His face was scrunched up, and he looked to be deep in thought.

"What is it?" Cooper asked.

"August."

"You mean Winchester?" Cooper smiled faintly.

"Whatever," Yancy replied sourly. "I can't believe August is Winchester. Our own cousin. You've heard the stories. He's killed folks out of pure meanness."

"I've heard that, yes."

"August was always a bit wild, but not *that* bad."

"It's been years since we've been around him," Cooper reminded. "Folks change."

"Well, there goes the Landon name," Yancy muttered. "It used to stand for something."

"You know how stories get worse each time they're told. Mebbe it's not as bad as it sounds."

Yancy snorted his response.

"Give Winchester a chance," Cooper continued. "With a little help from us, he might change."

Yancy scowled at that and changed the subject.

"I wonder what happened between him and Quincy."

"Sounds like they had a disagreement."

"Quincy was always calm, quiet, and collected," Yancy recalled. "Sorta like me. Only bigger."

"A *lot* bigger."

"Without Quincy's influence, that could be why August got so wild."

"Rondo was a mite wild too," Cooper reminded. "Look how he turned out."

Yancy took in a deep breath and exhaled as he thought on that.

"Yes," he said. "We did a good job with Rondo."

"We sure did. We arrested him, threw him in jail, and bribed him into giving up his partner and best friend," Cooper said, his face emotionless. "We taught him a thing or two."

"That ain't exactly how it happened," Yancy shot his brother a dark look.

"Mebbe not, but it still worked."

"And you think we should do the same thing for Winchester?"

"It's a thought."

"Well," Yancy looked considerate. "I could mention it to Judge Parker. There's plenty to arrest him on. We'd just need a warrant."

"It'd be for his own good," Cooper declared. "After all, we're family, and us Landons have always helped each other."

"He might not appreciate our method of help."

"Neither did Rondo, but look at the results."

Yancy nodded slowly.

"We'll keep it in mind," he said.

Cooper returned the nod, and they sat there a while in silence.

Finally, Yancy sighed again.

"That mule of yours," he complained.

"What about him?"

"The *one* time I wanted him to buck, and he acted like a kid horse."

Cooper chuckled.

"Yes, Jug-head can be hard to figure."

"I've never liked him."

"The mule, or August?"

"I meant Jug-head, but take your pick."

"Mebbe Jug-head just doesn't like us," Cooper suggested. "Even Kolorado swore he was kid gentle."

Yancy grunted at that.

"Mebbe you should sell him," he suggested.

"I have," Cooper reminded. "But..."

"He keeps coming back," Yancy finished the sentence, and Cooper nodded.

Chapter thirty-nine

Winchester led the way, and he set a hard, grueling pace.

The moon wasn't as full as it had been. However, it still gave off decent light, and Winchester could see his surroundings just fine.

The terrain was flat and sandy. There wasn't much grass, just some greasewood scattered about.

Winchester rode southwest to avoid the hill. They went several miles, and then he turned west towards the mountains.

The night passed quietly, and Winchester held the hard pace. Nobody said anything, and they followed each other in a long, single line.

Renewed vigor could be seen in Rondo, Lee, and Jeremiah. Their faces were stern with determination, and they rode with purpose.

As dawn arrived, they could tell that they were much closer to the mountains.

Winchester pulled up briefly. He looked thoughtful as he studied the countryside, and he turned to the north a bit.

They rode several more miles.

By midmorning, Winchester could feel Jug-head starting to labor. He pulled up, and everybody dismounted.

All the horses were breathing heavily, and they blew tiny flecks of foam from their nostrils. They were covered with sweat, and their flanks heaved.

"Reckon we'd best let them breathe a bit," Winchester suggested, and everyone nodded their agreement.

Winchester tied Jug-head to a shrub. He patted the sweaty mule on the rump, and then he walked forward and studied the mountains.

Lee came up beside him, holding a canteen. He took a deep swig, and then offered it to Winchester.

"Thanks," Winchester said, and he took several long swallows.

"We headed in the right direction?" Lee asked.

Winchester nodded and gestured.

"See that split in the mountains? That's the pass."

Lee nodded thoughtfully as he squinted ahead.

"It's a long ways, but we should reach the foothills before dark," Winchester said.

"Should, long as the horses don't play out," Lee agreed.

"We'll make it."

Lee nodded again, and it was silent for a moment.

"You really think we can catch those Apaches?" Lee finally asked.

"Normally, I'd say no," Winchester replied matter-of-factly. "But, the way this bunch is acting, mebbe. Most Apaches would ride up into the mountains, cover their tracks, and be gone. But, this bunch almost acts like they *want* to be found. Mebbe they're eager for more blood."

"Meaning ours?"

"You said it."

Lee frowned at that but didn't reply.

Several seconds passed, and Winchester glanced at Lee and changed the subject.

"I already know about Rachel," he said, and asked, "What about the other one? What's her name?"

"April."

"Yeah. Who does she belong to?"

A wistful look crossed Lee's face.

"Nobody, I reckon."

"But, you have feelings for her," Winchester guessed.

"I do."

"How 'bout him," Winchester jabbed a thumb in Jeremiah's direction. "Is he a brother or something?"

"Not hardly," Lee muttered. He hesitated, and said, "He has feelings for her too."

"Same sorta feelings you have?"

108

"Pretty much."

Winchester glanced at Jeremiah, and then at Lee.

"Oh boy," he said.

"You said it," Lee smiled.

Chapter forty

Midmorning found Yancy and Cooper several miles down the trail.

Yancy was irritated. Their pace had been slow, mainly because they'd been stopping every mile or so.

Cooper had a spyglass, and each time they halted he had carefully scanned the landscape. So far, all he'd seen was flat, desert terrain, jumping with heat waves.

"No hill?" Yancy asked after their latest stop.

"Not yet," Cooper shook his head.

"It would have been helpful if Winchester had mentioned how far this hill was."

"A small, forgotten detail."

Yancy grunted and said, "I hope he didn't forget to mention anything else."

"If he did, I have a feeling we'll find out," Cooper replied. "And soon."

Yancy grunted again while Cooper put away his eyeglass, and they trotted on. Cooper rode in front, and Yancy followed, leading No-see-ums.

"Been thinking," Yancy commented after a few minutes.

"You usually do," Cooper replied, and asked, "What about this time?"

"No Worries. It sure is peculiar that he's the one leading this raid."

"And you don't believe in coincidences."

"Not like this."

Cooper pinched his face in thought.

"After what you did to him, No Worries probably doesn't like us much," he said.

"How's that?"

"It'd be embarrassing, getting whopped on the head in your own tepee," Cooper explained. "Just imagine, a great war chief like him, trying to explain what happened."

"It must have been difficult for him."

"I'm sure," Cooper couldn't help but smile at the thought.

"And, before that, we left him six crates of useless rifles," Yancy recalled.

Cooper nodded and said, "I reckon we've earned the right to be disliked."

"At least a little."

"You think he did this to get even?" Cooper assumed.

"It's sure possible."

"How'd he know who we were?" Cooper objected.

"Somebody must've told him."

"How'd that happen?" Cooper raised an eyebrow. "You don't suppose he rode into the nearest town and asked somebody, real nice like?"

"No," Yancy scowled.

"Well then?"

"No Worries trades a lot," Yancy reminded. "Some Injun trader could have told him."

A thoughtful look crossed Cooper's face.

"That's actually possible," he admitted.

"And," Yancy continued, "instead of telling No Worries where *we* lived, he told him where Rondo lived."

"Be an easy mistake," Cooper said.

Yancy nodded, and several seconds passed as they thought on that.

"We could be wrong," Cooper finally said.

"Could be."

"But, you don't think we are."

"I don't."

"So, what are we going to do about it?"

"Ruin his plans, and get Rachel and April back," Yancy declared.

"Then what?"

"Right now, I'd settle for that."

Cooper nodded thoughtfully but didn't reply.

111

There was a small cluster of trees ahead. They rode up amongst them, and Cooper pulled up. Yancy came up beside him while he pulled out his eyeglass.

He squinted through it and slowly scanned the landscape. Suddenly, he set up straight in the saddle and gave a little grunt.

"Do you see a hill?" Yancy asked hopefully.

"I sure do."

"How far?"

"Hard to say. Several miles, anyway."

"See any Injuns?"

"Nope," Cooper replied. "But, it's brushy. Especially at the top."

"Must be it then."

Cooper lowered the eyeglass and nodded.

"I'd say so," he agreed.

"Any chance they could see us?"

"I doubt it, unless they have a spyglass stronger than mine."

"Well," Yancy looked thoughtful. "We'd best not ride any closer until we figure out what to do."

Cooper nodded again, and it was silent as they thought on the task at hand.

"Got any ideas?" Cooper asked.

"Well, I figure we should kill them before they kill us."

Cooper smiled faintly and said, "I don't reckon they'd want to surrender."

"You could ask, if you want."

"If I only spoke Apache-," Cooper's voice trailed off.

"Well, so much for that," Yancy replied, and said, "That means we'll have to kill them."

"Seems harsh," Cooper said distastefully.

"No way around it."

"Reckon not," Cooper agreed. A few moments passed, and he commented, "There's some that would object to this method of treatment."

"Who's that?"

"Fellers back east," Cooper explained. "They feel sorry for the Injuns. Claim they're getting a raw deal."

Yancy grunted at that.

"That's 'cause they've never been shot at by one."

"That does tend to change a feller's mind," Cooper agreed.

"And in a hurry," Yancy added.

Chapter forty-one

To save their horses' strength, Winchester slowed their pace that afternoon. The hot sun bore down unmercifully, and man and horse were both drenched with sweat.

The flat ground gave way to small hills as they neared the mountains, and it became rougher. There were also a few trees and some grass.

Not far from here was where Winchester's horse had gone down, and he looked wistful as he yearned for his saddle.

"Hot," Brian commented as they trotted along.

"Sure is," Lee agreed.

"Sticky as it is, you'd think it was going to rain," Rondo spoke up.

"Not likely," Winchester turned and looked back at everyone. "Doesn't rain much around these parts."

"I sorta guessed that," Lee said as he glanced at the dry, cracked ground.

Another hour passed, and they rode up to a dry gully. The walls were steep, and it looked sandy in the bottom.

"It's a mite rough traveling, but this draw goes all the way to the backside of that pass," Winchester announced. "Be a good spot to leave our horses."

"Are those walls climbable?" Rondo asked as he looked down.

"It's doable," Winchester replied. "It's not as steep a mile or two back to the east, but we ain't got the time to go back."

Everybody nodded, and Winchester slapped Jug-head on the rump, forcing him down the crumbling bank.

It was a steep descent, and Jug-head's rump almost touched the ground as they slid down.

Suddenly, Jug-head's front legs crumpled.

Winchester felt the mule falling, and he leaped spryly from his back. He landed on his feet and ran to escape being pinned.

Dust boiled as Jug-head rolled downwards, and he landed with a thump. A few seconds passed, and he struggled to his feet.

"Are you all right?" Rondo called down.

Winchester appeared from the boiling dust. He had lost his hat, and sand clung to the sweat on his face.

"I'm fine, but Jug-head ain't," he replied sourly.

"Did he break a leg?"

"No, he's just crippled."

"We'll be right down," Lee said.

"Good luck."

Lee glanced at everybody, and muttered, "Well, here goes."

He encouraged his horse forward, but the horse balked in protest. Lee frowned and raked his spurs along the horse's sides. This startled the horse, and he leaped involuntarily. Before he could stop, they were sliding downhill. They finally reached the bottom, and the horse staggered upright and took a few trembling steps.

"I made it!" Lee yelled up above.

Nobody else had any problems either, and they gathered around Winchester as he examined Jug-head.

Already, Jug-head's ankle was swelling. Winchester made him take a few steps, but he could barely put any weight on it.

"Well, he's done for," Winchester said, disappointment in his voice.

"You can ride double with me," Rondo offered.

"We aren't too far from that pass," Winchester replied. "I'll walk."

"What about Jug-head?" Rondo asked.

"Reckon I'll turn him loose. Tough as he is, he might make it."

115

Nobody had any better suggestion, so Winchester took the bridle off and gave Jug-head a slap on the rump.

"Good luck, mule," he said.

Jug-head seemed to understand, and he limped slowly down the gully, head down, headed east.

Everybody watched the mule a moment, and then Winchester walked over and grabbed his hat. He put it on and turned towards the mountains.

He held his rifle in one hand, and he slung his bridle over his shoulder.

"Let's go," he said, and he took off in a broken, relentless trot.

Chapter forty-two

"Only two options I can come up with," Yancy announced.

They were still a-horseback, in amongst the trees.

"Glad to know we have choices," Cooper replied. "What are they?"

"The less strategic thing to do would be to charge that hill and start shooting."

"Not much strategy in that," Cooper agreed.

"However," Yancy continued. "It's possible that one of them might jump on his pony and take out as soon as we're spotted."

"Can't let that happen," Cooper shook his head.

"That leaves us with the second option."

"Hope it's better than the first one."

"We wait until dark," Yancy said as he ignored Cooper's comment. "We leave our horses here, circle around on foot, sneak up behind them, and attack at dawn. 'Course, being on foot, we'll either kill them, or they'll kill us."

"I'd rather it be them."

"We agree on that."

"Lot could go wrong," Cooper reasoned. "Apaches are hard to sneak up on."

"I figured I'd leave my spurs here," Yancy offered.

"That's mighty considerate," Cooper said, and added, "You need moccasins. They're a lot quieter."

"I could wear one of yours."

Cooper grunted at that but didn't reply.

"So, you think we can pull this off?" Yancy asked.

"Without getting killed?"

"Might as well."

"Sure," Cooper said. "We'll just slip in there like a bar of soap, all slippery like."

Yancy turned in the saddle, looked at Cooper, and raised an eyebrow.

"Bar of soap?"

"I read it in a dime novel," Cooper explained with a sheepish grin.

"Didn't know you read dime novels."

"Wyatt and I've been reading them in the evenings. It's something we do together."

Yancy didn't reply for a moment.

Then he said, "Now I know why Wyatt spends a lot of time out at Tussle's ranch."

Cooper scowled, but didn't say anything.

Chapter forty-three

Even though he was on foot, Winchester still managed to set a brisk pace. He had remarkable endurance, and he never broke stride.

The gully narrowed as they neared the mountains. In some places, it was barely wide enough for a horse to squeeze through.

The walls were reddish clay, and several twisted, gnarled mesquites somehow managed to hang onto the sides.

Some of the roots were exposed where running water had washed away the soil, and Rondo gestured at that.

"Has to rain sometime," he said.

Lee nodded his agreement as he studied the eroded walls.

"I bet this little gully can flood in a hurry," he said. "Probably catches a lot of run off from the mountains."

"Looks like," Rondo agreed.

They reached the end of the draw right before dark. It mushroomed out, resembling a bowl, and made a natural corral for the horses.

"We'll take a short breather," Winchester announced. "From here, we go on foot."

Everybody dismounted, pulled out their rifles, and tended to their horses. After that, they grabbed their canteens and took several swigs.

Rondo rummaged through his saddlebags and found his moccasins. He pulled his boots off and slipped them on. They were a bit stiff, but they felt good.

Winchester looked slightly amused as he watched him. They were a short distance from the others, so he lowered his voice.

"Wear moccasins much?" He asked.

"Only when I'm traveling on foot," Rondo replied.

"Did Ben Kinrich teach you that?"

"Actually, Cooper did."

Winchester nodded. A few seconds passed, and he asked, "Spend much time with Yancy and Cooper?"

"Some. Especially these past few years."

"You get along?"

"Mostly."

Winchester nodded again, and said, "Yancy's never cared much for me."

"Why do you say that?"

"When we were younger, he hardly ever talked to me. And, the few times he did, I could always hear disapproval in his voice. Reminded me of my mother."

"Silence is Yancy's natural element," Rondo replied. "He only talks when he has something to say."

"Well, he always did have the personality of a wet mop," Winchester recalled. "Everything was a struggle for him, and he took things too personal."

"Still does," Rondo said.

"Not me. I enjoy life."

"Yancy does too," Rondo argued. "Just in a different way."

Winchester grunted at that and looked up at the sky.

"Well, time to move along," he announced, and he and Rondo joined the others.

"Bring your ropes," Winchester told everyone.

"What for?" Lee asked.

"You'll see."

Lee frowned at that, but he didn't reply as everybody pulled their ropes off their saddle.

Winchester turned and went down the gully a ways. He looked thoughtful as he searched for a spot to climb out, and everyone followed.

Chapter forty-four

To not move can be the hardest part, and Cooper and Yancy grew restless while they waited for darkness.

They tied their horses in amongst the trees, and then they sat on a downed tree trunk.

While they sat there, they noticed clouds forming over the mountains. They were fast building, and it wasn't long until thunderheads began boiling up.

"What do you make of that?" Cooper gestured.

"Looks like it might rain," Yancy observed. "Especially in the mountains."

"Sure does," Cooper agreed. He thought on that, and added, "Don't know if that's good or bad."

"Might be good," Yancy figured. "Those Injuns will be less watchful in a downpour."

"Worked for us," Cooper recalled.

"Sure did."

Cooper grinned as he recalled Lee's words.

"Who says you can't count on a thunderstorm," he said.

"Could miss us," Yancy warned.

"It's possible, but I don't think it will," Cooper replied as he studied the sky.

"We'll find out soon enough."

Cooper nodded, and it was quiet for a bit.

A half hour passed, and the sun disappeared behind the clouds.

"Well, looks like a pleasant evening shaping up," Cooper commented wryly.

"Nothing like a stroll in the rain," Yancy added.

Cooper smiled.

"You ready?"

"Ready as I'm going to be."

Cooper nodded and stood. He walked over to his horse, rummaged through his saddlebags, and pulled out his moccasins.

Yancy was a bit envious as he watched Cooper slip them on. He made the decision to make his own pair, just as soon as he could.

Cooper glanced at Yancy. He noticed his yearning look, but he didn't say anything.

Yet.

Chapter forty-five

Climbing out of the gully proved to be a difficult task.

The mesquite roots offered them something to cling to, and they managed to pull themselves along.

Everybody's muscles ached in protest as they reached the top. They dusted themselves off, and then they glanced up at the mountainside looming beside them.

"We've got to climb *that*?" Lee scowled.

"Yep," Winchester replied.

The way to the top was bare, rocky, wind blown, and sun baked.

"Not much cover," Lee observed.

"Nope," Winchester agreed, and added, "Let's get to it."

Lee looked disgruntled, but he didn't say anything. Winchester led the way, followed by Rondo, Brian, Jeremiah, and then Lee.

They were careful not to follow too close as they trudged upwards. Once Jeremiah slipped, but he managed to catch himself.

"You all right?" Lee asked from behind.

"Sure," Jeremiah replied, and added, "How 'bout you?"

"Never better," he grunted.

A few seconds passed, and Jeremiah said, "Been thinking."

"What about?"

"April."

"Really? So have I."

"I had a talk with Yancy, and he explained a few things," Jeremiah said. "He actually made sense."

Lee scowled at that.

"When did Yancy become such an expert?"

"We both want her to be happy," Jeremiah continued. "Am I correct?"

"You could say that."

"But, the decision is hers, not ours," Jeremiah said. "*If we all get out of this alive, I suggest we let her choose, and that'll be that.*"

"Sounds simple enough."

"So we agree?"

Lee thought for a moment.

"I think we do."

"Back in the old days, we would have probably shot each other," Jeremiah smiled.

"It's probable," Lee smiled with him.

"I'm glad we're mature enough to avoid trouble," Jeremiah said.

"Depends," Lee replied.

"On what?"

"Who she chooses."

Jeremiah chuckled. It was quiet for a moment, and he added, "There's something else to discuss."

"And what's that."

"The hotel."

"Yes, we should discuss that."

"It wouldn't be wise for us to work together. Might end up killing each other."

"Could be difficult," Lee agreed.

"I have a suggestion that will solve everything."

"Let's hear it."

"Whoever April chooses, gets the hotel," Jeremiah declared.

"Interesting concept," Lee replied as he thought on it.

"Is it a bet?"

"A bet?"

"Sure. We both bet on April, and the winner gets everything."

"What does the loser get?"

"Health," Jeremiah replied. "And, a fresh start elsewhere."

Lee frowned but didn't reply.

"That's the only way April can be happy," Jeremiah pointed out. "We both can't be in her life."

Lee nodded slowly in agreement.

"All right," he decided. "It's a bet."

"May the best man win," Jeremiah said, and it almost sounded like a prayer.

Chapter forty-six

Even Winchester felt a bit winded when they finally reached the top. He could feel the drag of exhaustion in his legs, and they trembled slightly.

The top of the pass was surprisingly narrow. The terrain was rocky and bare, except for some huge, round stones scattered about.

Brian was having the hardest time of them all. His face was drenched in sweat, and he was out of breath. A knifing pain from an old injury ripped at his side, and he limped noticeably.

Using his shirtsleeve, he wiped sweat and grime from his brow. He leaned against one of the stones, pulled the stopper from his canteen, and drank deeply.

"Oh man," he grumbled as water dribbled down his stubbled jaw. "This is rough country."

"And it gets rougher," Winchester informed.

Brian scowled at that. He took another swig, and then glanced around.

"I wonder how these big stones got up here," he said.

"Well, I was on one side-," Lee quipped.

"Sure you was," Brian said wryly.

"Look at that," Rondo suddenly said, and he gestured to the west.

Thunderheads boiled up high into the sky. It was dark blue underneath, and occasional lightning flashed.

They could also feel a slight, cool breeze. Hot as it was, it was welcome.

"I thought it didn't rain in these parts," Lee shot Winchester a dark look.

"Doesn't much," Winchester replied as he studied the clouds. "But, when it does, it pours."

"Wish I'd known that earlier," Lee muttered.

"Didn't think it mattered," Winchester shrugged.

"We left our horses down there in a hole," Lee reminded. "It wouldn't take much rain to flood that gully."

"It wouldn't," Winchester agreed, and added, "Those clouds are coming this way too."

"So now what?" Lee asked.

It was silent as everybody thought on that, and Rondo finally cleared his throat.

"I suggest Brian goes back," he said. "He can lead the horses out if need be."

"What about us?" Jeremiah spoke up.

"We'll catch up eventually," Rondo reasoned.

Jeremiah didn't look convinced, but he remained silent.

"Makes sense," Winchester said, and Lee nodded his agreement.

They looked at Brian, but he just glared at them.

"I have to go back?" He asked, displeasure in his voice.

"Can't lose the horses," Winchester pointed out.

"So I just climbed all the way up here for nothing?"

"Least it'll be easier going back down," Winchester tried to be helpful.

Brian's glare deepened, and he didn't reply.

Meanwhile, Lee walked over to the edge and looked down into the pass.

Just as Winchester had said, the pass was narrow and rocky. The walls were mostly all rock, and they were almost straight up and down.

"We have to go down *that*?" He objected.

"And back up again," Winchester added.

Lee looked doubtful, but he didn't say anything. Instead, he asked, "Where's that underground spring?"

"Back to the east," Winchester pointed.

"How far?"

"'Bout a mile, give or take."

"And that's where those Injuns should be camped."

"That's the hope."

"What if they aren't there?"

127

"Then we'll come up with another plan," Winchester replied, and he glanced at the sky. "Not much daylight left. It'd be best if we reached the bottom before dark."

Everybody nodded and moved to the edge. It was silent as they all looked down at the sharp descent.

"Oh, boy," Rondo finally said. "This should be fun."

Chapter forty-seven

"How are we supposed to get down there?" Jeremiah asked with a scowl.

"You'll see," Winchester replied, and added, "I'll need everybody's ropes."

Winchester was good with knots. He skillfully tied all the ropes together, and the end result was one, long rope.

He eyed a smaller, round rock that was near the edge. He put his shoulder against it and pushed mightily, but he couldn't budge it.

"It'll do," he said, satisfied.

He shook out a loop, tossed it around the rock, and pulled the loop tight. Then, he tossed the slack below.

To his satisfaction, the other end of the rope just reached the bottom.

"All set," he announced. He glanced at everyone and asked, "Who's first?"

"I can't hold onto the rope *and* my rifle," Rondo replied.

"I'll pass it down as soon as you reach the bottom," Winchester replied.

Rondo nodded somberly. He spat in his hands and rubbed them in some dirt. Then, he grabbed the rope and started down.

It would have been a nearly impossible task without the rope. However, Rondo was able to lean heavily against it, and it allowed him to keep his balance as he worked his way down.

It only took him a minute or two to reach the bottom. He quickly inspected the area, and then he waved up at Winchester.

Winchester signaled back and pulled up the rope.

"Give me your rifles," he told everyone.

There were four rifles, and Winchester tied them together skillfully. He grunted in satisfaction as he tightened the last knot.

Being as careful as he could, he lowered the rifles down to Rondo. Only once did the rifles scrape up against the side, and Lee and Jeremiah winced.

Rondo untied the rifles and waved, and Winchester turned to Jeremiah.

"Your turn," he said.

Jeremiah had no problems reaching the bottom, and neither did Lee.

Winchester was the last to go. He grabbed the rope and glanced at Brian.

"We'll be right back," he said.

"Good luck," Brian replied.

Winchester grinned recklessly as he started his descent.

Chapter forty-eight

"Did you know, it's almost impossible for moccasins to rub blisters?" Cooper asked as they walked along.

"You don't say."

"Boots can rub blisters in a hurry. Especially if you have to walk a long ways in sandy, desert country."

"Uh-huh."

"But not moccasins. I could go all day and not rub even one little blister."

"You go ahead and do that."

Cooper chuckled, and it was silent for a bit.

They had been walking for an hour. It was now completely dark, and the temperature had cooled considerably.

Even though it was dark, Cooper had no difficulties seeing the way to go. The thunderstorm in the mountains flashed lightning every few moments, and it lit up the ground for a split second each time.

They went southwest a ways, and then Cooper headed straight for the mountains.

Another hour passed, and Cooper stopped to get his bearings. Each time lightning flashed, he took a quick look around.

"How far you reckon we've gone?" He asked.

"I figured we would have hit the ocean by now," Yancy gasped as he caught his breath.

Cooper smiled faintly and said, "Reckon we've traveled two miles?"

"At least."

"Well," Cooper looked considerate. "If we've gone that far, we should have passed that hill by now. We need to cut back to the north and come in behind them."

Yancy nodded, and they trudged along.

"This desert country looks all the same to me," Yancy commented as he looked around.

"Does."

"I hope you know where you're going."

"I think I do."

"It'll be embarrassing if we walk back up to our horses in a while."

Cooper smiled in the darkness.

"I won't tell anybody if you don't," he said.

Yancy grunted, and it fell silent as they ambled on.

Chapter forty-nine

They worked their way down the pass with care and patience.

Winchester went first, followed by Rondo. Lee and Jeremiah lagged behind, and they kept a keen eye on their back trail.

It was now dark, and the air was remarkably cool. There was also a rumble in the clouds, and they could feel moisture in the air. Occasional lighting struck the ground behind them, and the flashes lit up the pass for a split second each time.

Winchester stopped abruptly, and Rondo almost bumped into him.

"Look," he said softly as Lee and Jeremiah came up beside them.

Down in the pass, they could see the flickering of campfires. The flames reflected off the steep walls, and it resembled a fiery bowl.

"Well," Winchester said, his voice flat. "There they are."

"Let's go," Rondo urged.

"Easy now," Winchester cautioned.

Rondo nodded, and Winchester led out.

They moved at an even slower pace.

The ground was mainly open, but Winchester managed to take advantage of what little cover the pass offered. He moved from rock to rock, tree to tree, and the others followed close behind him.

As they got closer, Winchester spotted a big, flat rock just above the Indian's camp that was nestled against the wall. It offered a good vantage point, and Winchester worked his way to the backside of it.

They were so close they could hear the murmur of the Apache's conversation, and everybody's face was tense with anticipation.

Winchester planned on scouting the camp alone, but Rondo pulled himself up on the rock before Winchester could tell everyone.

Winchester scowled. He motioned for Lee and Jeremiah to wait, and he crawled after Rondo.

Pressing himself as flat as possible, Rondo inched forward until he could see their camp. He felt some movement, and Winchester crawled up beside him.

There were four campfires spread about in front of them, and Indians were gathered around three of them. A carcass of a horse was on the other side of camp, and they could smell meat cooking.

The empty campfire was the closest.

At first glance it looked like there was nobody there, but then Winchester caught a glimpse of Rachel and April.

They sat on the ground beside each other, their backs toward them. Their heads were close together, and it looked like they were talking.

Rondo spotted them a split second later, and Winchester felt his body jerk and flinch beside him.

Winchester laid a comforting and restraining hand on his shoulder. Rondo didn't look at him, but Winchester could tell that he relaxed a bit.

Suddenly, as if Rachel knew they were there, she turned and looked in their direction. Her face had a yearning look, and Winchester felt Rondo's muscles grow rigid.

"Easy now," Winchester whispered softly.

Rondo didn't reply, and he kept his eyes fastened to Rachel.

Winchester heard a noise. Some Indians were walking up from the other side of camp, and Winchester and Rondo ducked.

The Indians carried branches and brush, and they piled it up against the wall of the pass.

Winchester watched them work, and he figured they were making a lean-to of some sort, getting prepared for the rain.

Winchester had seen enough. He tugged on Rondo's shoulder, and then he pushed himself backwards. Rondo followed, and they joined the others behind the rock.

Big, wet raindrops started to fall as Winchester motioned everybody close.

He spoke in a soft, hushed voice, and Lee and Jeremiah's eyes lit up when he told them how close Rachel and April were.

"Those Injuns are settling in, getting ready for the rain," Winchester continued. "They ain't as watchful as they'd normally be."

"What's the plan?" Rondo hissed.

Winchester studied his eager face for a moment.

"You reckon you could sneak up behind Rachel and April?" He asked.

"Without being seen?"

"Be helpful," Winchester replied. "If not, Lee, Jeremiah, and I will be up on that rock, ready to cover you. Soon as you're spotted, we'll open up. It'll be up to you to get Rachel and April out of there."

Rondo was quiet as he thought on that, and then he nodded.

"I can do it."

"Good boy," Winchester said. "Wait until we're in position, and then go for it."

Rondo nodded again, and Winchester climbed the rock again and inched forward. Jeremiah followed, but Lee held back.

"Luck, Button," Lee said softly.

Rondo grinned briefly.

"Thanks."

Lee nodded. He patted Rondo on the shoulder encouragingly, and then he crawled up after the others.

The rock wasn't very wide, and Lee had to wiggle up between Jeremiah and Winchester.

All three held their rifles, and they eased back the hammers, careful not to make much noise. Then, they waited for Rondo to make his move.

Chapter fifty

Brian was exhausted, and he saw no need to hurry.

After the others left, he sat and leaned against a big rock. He decided he'd catch his breath, and then climb back down to the horses.

He flexed his cramped muscles while he rested.

"I'm getting too old for this," he said out loud.

He leaned his head back and closed his eyes. He could feel sweat trickling down his back, and his side continued to throb.

"Just a few minutes more," he told himself.

The next thing he knew, he bolted awake as lightning struck nearby. Seconds later, a deep rumble came from the clouds.

It was raining big drops, and his shirt was already damp. He scowled and scrambled to his feet.

Brian had no idea how much time had passed, and he was furious with himself for falling asleep. However, dwelling on it wouldn't do any good, so he focused on the task at hand.

He grabbed his rifle and took out. The lightning was very close, and he wanted off the high ground as fast as possible.

He was halfway down when the rain became a torrid downpour. It felt like buckets of water being poured on his head, and Brian was soaked within seconds.

Vision became horrible. The ground was slick, and Brian had a hard time keeping his balance. Several times he lost his footing, and he hit the ground on his backside and slid several feet.

Brian finally reached the bottom, and he was surprised at how deep the running water already was. He made his way over to the edge of the gully and looked down.

Lightning flashed, and he could see the horses. They were spooked and moving all about.

Water was pouring into the gully, and the current was remarkably strong. It pulled at Brian, and he had a hard time keeping his footing.

He bent over and reached for a mesquite root. His fingers wrapped around the gnarly root, but suddenly the bank crumbled underneath him. He fell straight down, and he uttered a startled yell.

He made a big splash as he landed in the bottom of the gully. He was on his back, and his rifle landed near him.

The cold water shocked him, but he still managed to grab his rifle. Then, he struggled to his feet.

The swirling water was already knee deep, and Brian could tell that it was rising fast.

He sloshed over to the horses. They were terrified, and he spoke soothing words to them.

He slid his rifle in his scabbard. Then, working as fast as he could, he tethered the horses into one, long line. The horses were jumpy, and Brian experienced great difficulty.

He finally finished, and he sloshed over to his horse. He mounted, grabbed the lead rope, and kicked up his horse.

The terrified horses didn't want to follow, and Brian had to take a dally around his saddle horn. He pulled them along a ways until they finally started to follow.

Their hooves sunk in the mud with each step, and travel was extremely slow.

Brian could almost touch the running water with his boots, and he swallowed uneasily as he watched the water swirl around them.

"We have to get out of this draw," he told the horses. "And in a hurry!"

Chapter fifty-one

Another hour came and went, and Yancy and Cooper were now walking back towards the east.

The thunderstorm behind them was impressive. Lightning danced across the sky, and they could feel the moisture from it. There was also an occasional deep rumble of thunder.

Each time lightning flashed, they glanced around quickly, searching for the hill. So far, all they'd seen was flat, sandy ground.

"We've walked in a big circle," Yancy said sourly.

"That was the plan," Cooper reminded.

"So where's this hill?"

"In front of us," Cooper replied. A few seconds passed, and he added, "I think."

Yancy grunted. Lightning struck again, and they quickly inspected the area before the light faded.

"I'm starting to think we should have gone with the first option," Yancy said.

"The less strategic one?"

"Not much strategy walking in circles either."

"We'll find it," Cooper replied.

Yancy grunted again, and they walked on.

Another half hour passed, and the lightning never let up.

Yancy was about to say something when Cooper stopped abruptly. He knelt down, and Yancy hunkered beside him.

"See it?" Yancy asked in a whisper.

Cooper nodded and pointed.

"To the left," he said softly.

Yancy nodded back, but didn't say anything.

Voices had a way of traveling at nighttime, so there would be no talking now.

Taking their time, they edged toward the hill. The distance was several hundred yards, and it took them half an hour to reach it.

As they got closer, they pulled out their knives. They held their rifles in one hand, and their knives in the other as they crawled forward.

They crossed a clear, open spot and came up behind a sandy dune. Lightning flashed, and Cooper spotted three Indian ponies tied to trees beside the tank of water.

Cooper glanced at Yancy. He'd seen them too, and he nodded.

Cooper turned and studied the ground in front of them.

There were some thick, bushy shrubs off to the side. Cooper gestured at them, and they crawled up amongst them, being careful to avoid any thorns.

Lightning flashed, and they spotted two Indians at the top of the hill. They had dug in behind some brush, and their backs were to them.

Cooper glanced at Yancy. He held up two fingers, and Yancy nodded.

Cooper frowned his disappointment, and then he looked back up the hill.

They didn't move for a long time. Each time lightning flashed they searched all around them, but the third Indian failed to show himself.

Cooper finally decided that they needed another viewpoint. He glanced at Yancy and gestured at a pile of rocks a short distance away.

Yancy looked and nodded.

Cooper made a motion for Yancy to stay where he was. Yancy understood, and he nodded his agreement.

Cooper returned the nod, and he crawled forward while Yancy covered him.

He was halfway to the rocks when they heard a noise of moving feet.

Before they could react, the third Apache trotted up behind them.

Yancy was flat on the ground, lying on his stomach, between two thick shrubs. His feet were stuck out behind him, and the Apache tripped on his leg.

They heard a surprised grunt, and then the Apache yelled at the top of his voice when he spotted Yancy.

His hand went to his waist, and Yancy saw him raise his tomahawk. With a look of hatred, the Apache leaped forward and attacked.

Chapter fifty-two

Rondo was anxious, but he forced himself to be calm. He moved at a snail's pace as he crawled forward.

The rain was falling harder. The campfires smoked and hissed as they died, and the pass became darker.

The Indians hardly paid any notice to the captives. All their attention was on building a lean-to as quickly as possible.

The darkness pleased Rondo. And, any noise he made blended perfectly with the storm.

He was near soaked as he came up behind Rachel and April. They sat huddled together, a blanket wrapped around them, shivering in the rain.

"Rachel," he said softly.

She didn't hear him.

Rondo inched closer, and he reached out and touched her on the shoulder.

She jumped, but he calmed her quickly.

"It's me, Rondo!" He hissed.

Rachel couldn't believe her ears, and she glanced wide-eyed at April. Her senses reeled, and she started to turn around.

"Stay still! Both of you!" Rondo hissed.

Rachel nodded numbly. She wanted to cry as she clutched April's arm.

"Are you both all right?"

They nodded.

"Good. We're going to try and reach that big rock behind us. Can you do that?"

Again, they nodded.

"All right. Don't make any sudden moves. Stand slowly, and move back. Any shooting starts, run for that rock. Let's go."

Standing as one, they took small steps back. Rondo kept his hand on Rachel's shoulder as he guided them.

Across the camp, No Worries was busy supervising the hastily built lean-to. They needed more cover for the roof, and his eyes surveyed the surrounding area for anything useful.

He spotted the captives up and moving, and he uttered a surprised grunt. He squinted against the darkness as he watched them.

Was that a darker figure looming behind them?

Lightning flashed, and No Worries' eyes grew wide. He gave an Apache yell and leaped toward his rifle.

Chapter fifty-three

Yancy was out of position to grab his Colt, and he didn't have the time to swing his rifle up.

As the Apache swung down with his tomahawk, Yancy flipped over onto his back. He managed to block the blow with his forearm and knife.

Yancy was pinned. The Apache raised his tomahawk for another blow, and Yancy struggled mightily.

A rifle shot from Cooper bellowed out, followed by the thumping sound of a bullet hitting flesh. The Apache's body was flipped over backwards. He hit the ground on his back, kicked out, and was still.

With his rifle in hand, Cooper spun back around.

The two remaining Apaches were bent over, running down the hill. The closest warrior snapped off a shot, and Cooper heard a sharp whistling sound as the bullet fanned air close by his head.

Cooper returned the gunfire. He saw the Apache's body jerk, but he never broke stride as both Apaches disappeared into the darkness.

Cooper took a quick look over his shoulder.

Yancy was getting untangled from the shrubs. He grabbed his rifle and joined Cooper.

"You all right?" Cooper asked.

"I'm fine."

Cooper nodded, relieved.

"I heard shots," Yancy said. "Did you get one?"

"No. Just nicked him."

"You must be slipping," Yancy scolded.

Cooper shot his brother a dark look.

"I did just save your life," he reminded.

"I didn't say you were falling completely apart," Yancy said as he squinted into the darkness. "Where'd they go?"

"That way," Cooper gestured.

"Think they'll be back?"

"I figure they will. They'll want their horses."

Yancy nodded his agreement.

"Can't let them have 'em," he declared.

"I know," Cooper replied, and they made their way over to the dirt tank.

There was plenty of cover. They positioned themselves on either side of the horses, and they watched and waited with keen eyes. Each time lightning flashed, they quickly searched all around them.

A few minutes passed, and Cooper chuckled gruffly.

"What's so funny?" Yancy asked in a hushed voice.

"The hunters have just become the hunted," Cooper explained in a whisper.

"It appears so," Yancy whispered back.

Chapter fifty-four

As the campfires flickered out from the rain, Winchester lost track of Rondo. So he watched the captives instead, and his keen eyes caught some movement as Rondo crawled up behind them.

"He's there," Winchester whispered.

Lee and Jeremiah nodded.

The pouring rain had already soaked them. However, they ignored the storm as they focused their full attention on the Apaches.

From the corner of his eye, Winchester saw Rachel and April stand and step back.

He expected them to be spotted any second now, and he gripped his rifle in anticipation.

A loud war cry suddenly sounded out, and the Apaches stirred like a nest of hornets.

Winchester drew a bead on an Apache running toward the captives. He let out his breath and pulled the trigger.

The driving impact of the bullet struck the Apache in his torso. He took one more small, jerky step, and then fell as his knees buckled.

Lee and Jeremiah opened fire, and flame exploded from their rifles as they fired one shot after another. Below them, Rachel, April, and Rondo made it to safety behind the rock.

The Apaches were taken by complete surprise, and several warriors fell as they grabbed their rifles.

The rain fell harder, and it became a drenching downpour. However, Winchester, Lee, and Jeremiah kept up the furious gunfire as they sprayed the pass with bullets.

More Apaches fell, and they had no choice but to retreat.

But they couldn't leave the horses. So, while a few returned the gunfire, the rest grabbed the horses and led them down the pass. Then, the few Apaches that remained withdrew after them, still firing their rifles. However, none of the shots came close.

The Apaches disappeared into the darkness, and Winchester made a motion to quit firing.

"They've had enough!" He shouted through the rain.

"Now what?" Jeremiah yelled back.

"We get out of here!"

Lee and Jeremiah nodded. They reloaded their rifles, and then they stood and started to turn.

Lightning suddenly flashed.

They didn't know it, but an Apache had stayed below. He was crouched behind the lean-to, and he held his rifle ready as he waited for a shot.

The Apache caught a glimpse of figures on the flat rock. He aimed and fired, and he grunted in satisfaction when he heard the loud thump of a bullet hitting flesh.

Chapter fifty-five

To Brian's relief, the rain lightened as he rode east. There was still swirling water all around them, but the horses had calmed down some.

Brian was wet, cold, muddy, and miserable. He shivered in the saddle, and the horses struggled through the thick mud.

He figured he had gone maybe two miles when he spotted an opening in the steep wall of the gully. He pulled up and inspected it, and he figured the bank had crumbled from water pouring in.

He frowned thoughtfully, and he nodded as he came to a decision.

He rode in as close as he could and dismounted.

The bank was slick, and he had difficulty climbing it. He yanked on the reins, and his horse reluctantly followed.

Some of the horses down the line balked in protest, but they had no choice but to follow the next horse.

The last horse finally climbed out, and Brian heaved a sigh of relief. They were still in running water, but it wasn't nearly as deep.

Brian sloshed over to his horse, stepped into the saddle, and then sat there a moment. Each time lightning flashed, he studied his surroundings.

He was beside a tall mountain, and he figured the pass was on the other side.

He knew Winchester and the others would be coming from the west, so he turned back and followed the gully. He was careful to keep some distance between him and the crumbling bank.

The rain was hitting him in the face now. And, even though the rain had lightened, the horses didn't like riding into it. Brian had to take another dally around the saddle horn and drag them along, and travel was slow.

An hour passed.

By now the gully and mountain had drawn closer together, leaving a narrow ledge for Brian to go down.

He didn't want to chance falling into the gully. He rode in as close as he dared, and then he pulled up. He dismounted, checked on the horses, and sat on a nearby tree trunk.

"Now we wait," he told the horses, and he hunched his shoulders against the light rain.

Chapter fifty-six

As soon as they were concealed behind the rock, Rondo and Rachel embraced. Tears ran down her face, and they held each other fiercely.

Winchester, Lee, and Jeremiah were firing one gunshot after another, but Rondo couldn't let go just yet.

"Are you all right?" Rondo asked, his face anxious.

"I'm fine," Rachel said.

"Are you sure?"

"Yes, we're all right. Both of us."

Rondo was flooded with relief, and he hugged her even tighter.

"Is June all right?" April spoke up anxiously.

"She's fine," Rondo reassured. "She's with the Tomlins."

April looked relieved, and Rondo looked down at Rachel.

"I'm sorry it took us so long," he murmured. "We got here fast as we could."

"I knew you would come for us," Rachel said, and her eyes shown brightly at him.

The rain was easing up. They were soaked, but Rondo and Rachel didn't care as they held each other.

Rondo finally released her and turned, ready to lend a hand. However, the gunfire had stopped, and the others were climbing off the rock.

Lightning flashed. A rifle shot bellowed out, and Rondo heard the thumping sound of a bullet hitting flesh.

Both Lee and Jeremiah fell. Lee landed on his feet and sprinted forward to keep his balance, but Jeremiah landed in a heap.

Winchester slid down behind them, and everybody gathered around Jeremiah.

They propped him against a ragged boulder. Blood was already staining the front of his shirt, and his face was chalky as he grasped his belly with both hands.

"Take it easy now," Lee urged.

April uttered a gasp of despair as she knelt and examined the wound. He was gut shot, and blood was going everywhere.

Tears streamed down her face. She looked up at everybody for help, but they just stood there, their faces solemn.

Winchester glanced at Lee and Rondo. Without saying a word, he turned and slipped around the big rock to keep watch.

Jeremiah took in a few deep breaths, and his body trembled in shock.

"How 'bout this?" He said, his voice shaky.

"Don't talk," April encouraged. "Save your strength."

"For what?" Jeremiah gasped. "I'm gut shot."

"We'll carry you out," Lee spoke up.

Jeremiah shook his head and gasped.

"That would slow you down."

"You want us to leave you here?" April asked, her eyes wide.

"What I want," Jeremiah paused for a sharp pain to pass, "is for you to get out."

He raised a bloody hand before she could say anything.

"I'm dying," he said matter-of-factly.

April sobbed in protest, and Jeremiah looked at Lee.

"I fold," he said.

"What?" Lee didn't understand.

"Our bet," Jeremiah reminded. "You win. I fold."

Lee nodded but didn't reply.

"Take care of her," Jeremiah said, and his voice trembled again.

"I will," Lee promised softly.

Jeremiah nodded and looked back at April, who was still sobbing gently.

He reached out and ran his finger down her cheek.

"Don't cry for me," he said. "I want you to get out of here and live a long, happy life. You hear me?"

April managed to nod.

"All right then," Jeremiah said, and he glanced at Rondo and Lee. "Get me on that rock, and I'll hold 'em for as long as I can."

They nodded somberly. Being as gentle as possible, they picked him up. The pain was severe, and Jeremiah cried out.

They pushed him up onto the rock. Lee and Rondo crawled up beside him, and Rondo handed him his rifle.

"Might leave some extra cartridges," Jeremiah gasped.

Lee reached in his pocket and gave him a handful.

"I'll put them to good use," Jeremiah said, his face pale as he pulled out his Colt and placed it beside him for easy access.

"I'd save the last bullet in that six-shooter," Rondo said quietly so the women couldn't hear. "You don't want to be taken alive."

"I know."

Winchester hurried around the rock, and he looked up at them.

"Let's go!" He hissed.

Rondo and Lee didn't move as they looked down at Jeremiah. Both felt horrible, and it showed on their faces.

"Go on," Jeremiah told them. "Get April out."

"You're a good man," Lee said, his voice husky.

"No, I'm not," Jeremiah replied plainly. "But, I do good things occasionally. Now get."

Rondo and Lee nodded slightly. They took one last look at him, and then they slid off the rock.

Rondo took Rachel's hand, and Lee grabbed April's. They followed after Winchester in a brisk trot.

Minutes later, they heard gunfire erupt behind them as Jeremiah began his last stand.

Chapter fifty-seven

Yancy and Cooper continued to wait with nervous anticipation. They didn't talk, and the only thing that moved were their eyes.

The storm in the mountains wasn't as severe now. There wasn't as much lightening either, but Cooper couldn't decide if that was to their advantage or not.

They strained their ears as they listened for anything suspicious. The sounds of the night were loud, and frogs croaked around them. Cooper found that odd, because the rain had missed them.

A flash of lightening struck in the distance, and Cooper caught a glimpse of a running form.

It was the wounded Apache. He was hunched over, moving fast, and Cooper spotted the gleam of a knife.

Cooper was surprised at how close he was. He uttered a startled yell as he swung his rifle up.

He didn't take the time to aim. Instincts took over, and he fired from the hip.

The racing Apache broke stride, recovered, and continued his charge. His knife was raised, and the Apache's face was twisted with hate.

He uttered a high-pitched war cry, and Cooper pulled the trigger again.

To Cooper's amazement, this time the Apache didn't even flinch.

Cooper fired yet again, and the bullet hit the Apache squarely in the chest. He jerked under the impact and dropped the knife, but his churning legs carried him even closer.

The Apache fell only a few feet from Cooper. He kicked out, made some groaning sounds, and died.

Meanwhile, Yancy palmed his Colt and spun around.

At the same instant, the second Apache leaped from the darkness. He held a tomahawk, and he took a swing at Yancy's head.

Yancy ducked as the Apache raced forward. The tomahawk missed, and they collided hard. They fell backwards and made a big splash in the tank.

They thrashed in the water as they fought each other.

The Apache tried to swing his tomahawk, but Yancy grabbed his wrist. Meanwhile, Yancy reached down with his other hand and pulled out his knife.

The next few seconds were quick and violent. It was a hard, close fight, but Yancy finally prevailed. The Apache sank limply into the water while Yancy struggled to his feet.

Cooper stood beside the bank, rifle in hand, watching for an opportunity to fire.

"You all right?" Cooper called out.

"Sure, long as I don't drown."

"This is no time for a swim."

Yancy glared at Cooper as he drug the Indian to the side.

"Give me a hand," he said sourly. "I don't want this Injun bleeding in our drinking water."

Cooper reached down, grabbed the Apache's arm, and helped drag him up to dry ground.

"You're bleeding," Cooper gestured at Yancy's arm.

"It's nothing."

"Doesn't look like nothing."

"I bruise easily," Yancy replied.

Chapter fifty-eight

Gunfire blasted behind them, and it was especially loud in the narrow pass. Occasionally it faded, but then it returned a few seconds later.

Jeremiah was giving them precious time, and Winchester was determined to take advantage of it. His long, reaching strides quickly took him down the pass, and the others followed close behind.

The rope was still dangling where they'd left it. Everybody gathered around it, and they panted a few moments while they caught their breath.

"We have to climb *that*?" Rachel asked, her eyes wide as she glanced upward.

"Nothing to it," Winchester said, and he looked at Rondo. "You and Rachel go first. While you're climbing, I'll tie the rifles together. Soon as you reach the top, you can pull 'em up."

Rondo nodded and grabbed the rope.

April was worried for Rachel and her baby, but she didn't say anything. Now was not the time.

Rachel was worried too, but she grit her teeth in determination and looked at Rondo.

"I'm ready," she said.

"Good girl," Rondo said as he wrapped an arm around her. "We'll climb together. Understand?"

She nodded, and they started up.

It was a hard, difficult climb, and the rope bit into Rondo's hands.

They were halfway up when Rachel's legs gave way. She grimaced as she slid downwards.

Rondo caught her slim body, and he held on tightly as she got her legs back under her.

"You all right?" He asked, concern in his voice.

"I'm fine," Rachel said. "Let's go."

Rondo nodded. Gripping the rope, they proceeded upwards.

Below them, Lee and April watched with concern. Meanwhile, Winchester gathered the rifles and tied them together.

Lee glanced at April, and tears were still streaming down her face.

"Are you all right?" He asked.

She nodded, and explained, "I keep thinking about Jeremiah. I feel so bad for him."

Lee nodded somberly.

"I know," he said softly. "But, that's just the way it is."

"How's that?"

Lee paused while he gathered his words.

"We've all been around death since before the war. I reckon we're just used to it. The life we live, we know death could come for us anytime. We sorta expect it; that way we aren't so surprised when it happens."

"But how do you get used to it?" April asked, her eyes wide.

"Repetition helps."

April shuddered at the thought.

"You live a hard life."

"It's a hard country," Lee replied.

The gunfire down the pass stopped abruptly. Several seconds passed, but there was only an eerie silence.

Lee and April glanced at each other, and then they looked at Winchester.

He was paying them no attention as he squinted upwards.

"They made it," he said, and then he called out, "Pull the rifles up!"

Rondo's head appeared from above. He grabbed the rope, and the rifles jerked as they went up the slope. Rondo untied them and tossed the rope back down.

Winchester turned to Lee and April.

"Your turn," he said.

Lee nodded. He grabbed the rope, wrapped an arm around April, and started upwards.

"And hurry," Winchester added tersely.

Chapter fifty-nine

"How's your arm?" Cooper asked Yancy.

"Hurts a little."

"Too bad Josie isn't here," Cooper replied. "She could patch you up in no time."

Yancy grunted at that.

"No thanks."

"You'd rather bleed?"

"Yep. I've seen her work."

Cooper smiled faintly, and it was quiet while they assessed the situation.

"According to my precise calculations, I figure they should be here sometime tomorrow," Cooper announced. "Probably in the late afternoon. That, or possibly tomorrow evening."

"You call that precise?"

"So that gives us tonight and tomorrow to get ready," Cooper said as he ignored Yancy's sarcasm.

"What do you have in mind?"

"Well, first thing, one of us should fetch our horses," Cooper suggested. "Then, we should bury *them*." He gestured at the dead Apaches.

"Then what?"

"In the morning, we could clear a little brush around the hill. Mebbe set a trap."

"Trap?"

"Sure," Cooper nodded. "Been thinking. Without horses, those Apaches couldn't follow us. They'd have to turn back."

"Sounds good in theory."

"You remember how we ran off those horses during the war?"

Yancy nodded slowly.

"It was Chino's idea," he recalled. "It's actually an old Injun trick."

"And it worked."

"Sure did."

"It would work again," Cooper suggested. "Especially around here. Sandy as it is, we'd have no trouble digging a hole."

"It would be risky," Yancy warned.

"Risky is my middle name."

Yancy scowled.

"You're sounding like Winchester now."

Cooper grinned.

"I say we look around in the morning, and see if we can find a good spot," he suggested.

"We'll give it careful consideration," Yancy agreed.

Cooper nodded and turned towards the Indian ponies.

"I'll fetch the horses," he offered, and Yancy nodded.

He examined the Indian ponies, and he was pleasantly surprised. One was a spotted paint, but the other two were sorrels.

"These two sorrels have brands on them," he announced.

"Recognize the brands?" Yancy asked.

"Nope."

"Well, no telling where they came from. Apaches probably stole them in some raid."

"They seem gentle," Cooper remarked. "There's also some saddle marks on their backs."

"Gentle horses could come in handy."

"Sure could," Cooper agreed. "Especially since we didn't bring extra horses for Rachel and April."

A surprised look crossed Yancy's face, and he uttered a soft grunt.

"We didn't, did we."

"Just a small, forgotten detail," Cooper smiled.

Chapter sixty

Winchester grew impatient as he watched Lee and April climb. Their progress was slow, and April slipped and slid backwards several times.

Winchester yearned for his rifle, and he felt helpless without it. Any second Indians could appear, and all he had was his Colt.

Meanwhile, up above, Rondo grabbed his rifle. He walked over to the edge, leaned against a rock, and kept watch below. Rachel came up beside him, and she rested her head on his shoulder.

Rondo patted her on the back, but his eyes never left the pass.

"I'm proud of you," he said. "You've carried yourself well."

Rachel smiled at her husband.

"I had no choice," she replied. "I knew you were coming. I just had to keep it together until you reached us."

"I'm sorry it took so long."

"Where *have* you been?" Rachel asked, suddenly curious.

"J.T. Tussle needed help. I had to stay a few extra weeks."

"You could have written a letter!" Rachel scolded gently. "Why, I could have been dead!"

Rondo thought on that before he replied.

"If you were dead," he said. "What good would a letter have been?"

Rachel tried to frown at him, but she was so happy she couldn't.

Chapter sixty-one

Lee and April finally reached the top, and Lee's muscles ached in protest as they pulled themselves over onto the ledge.

Winchester was watching from below, and he grunted in satisfaction and grabbed the rope.

He started his ascent with ease. His strong arms pulled him along, and he had no problems as he scaled the wall.

Rondo's rifle barked as Winchester reached the ledge. He pulled himself over, rolled over onto his back, and pulled the rope up behind him.

"What are you shooting at?" Winchester asked.

"Saw some movement," Rondo replied as he squinted below.

While Lee and Rondo kept watch, Winchester pulled the loop off the rock and coiled the rope.

"See anymore movement?" Winchester asked as he looped the rope around his shoulder.

"Nope," Rondo shook his head.

"Then let's go," Winchester urged. "I doubt they can climb the wall, but I wouldn't count on it. We need to reach our horses."

Rondo and Lee nodded. They left the edge, grabbed Rachel and April's hand, and followed after Winchester.

"Sure is wet," Rondo said as they stumbled downward in a broken trot.

"Is," Winchester agreed.

"Hope that gully didn't flood."

"We'll know soon," Winchester grunted back.

The ground was slick, and Rachel and April slipped several times. But, Rondo and Lee were quick to catch them, and they finally reached the bottom.

They stood in running water. It was muddy, and they sank with each step.

Winchester struggled over to the edge of the gully and looked down.

"The horses!" He shouted. "They're gone!"

Lee and Rondo were startled.

"Where'd they go?" Lee asked.

"Brian must have led them out."

"Now what?" Rondo asked.

Winchester jabbed a thumb towards the east.

"We'll go that way."

Chapter sixty-two

It didn't take long for Rachel and April to become exhausted as they struggled through the water and mud. But, neither one said anything.

They went about a mile, and Winchester suddenly yelled and pointed ahead.

"There he is!"

"Thanks goodness!" Rachel cried out, and they quickened their steps.

Brian heard them coming, and he was relieved to see them.

"Where have you been?" Brian scolded. "You said you'd be right back."

"Time flies," Winchester replied.

Brian was about to reply when he spotted Rachel and April. His scowl turned into a wide grin, and he forgot all about his own troubles.

"You made it," he said softly.

"We did," Rachel returned the smile.

"How about that," Brian said, deeply pleased. He glanced around and asked, "Where's Jeremiah?"

"He didn't," Rondo said.

Brian frowned at that, but didn't say anything.

"Why are you so muddy?" Lee asked as he studied his soaked clothes.

"It happens," Brian replied, his face emotionless.

"You look like you've been wallowing around in it," Lee replied.

Brian didn't say anything. He stared at Lee, and his stern look suggested they should talk about something else.

Lee smiled faintly and asked, "Did Jug-head make it out?"

"Didn't see him."

"No sign at all?"

"I was busy," Brian replied.

While they talked, Winchester quietly assessed the situation.

"Hate to break up the chit-chat, but we'd better git," he spoke up. "I'll ride Jeremiah's horse, and the girls can ride double with Rondo and Lee."

Everybody nodded their agreement, and they moved to their horses.

April joined Lee. He wrapped his arm around her waist, and he felt a slight, thrilling feeling.

He picked her up with ease and placed her behind the saddle, and then he reluctantly withdrew his arm. However, April reached out and grabbed his hand.

Lee was surprised, and he looked up into her eyes. She was staring intently at him, and Lee's heart leaped.

"April-," he started to say.

"Yes?"

Lee didn't reply. They just looked at each other, and several seconds passed.

Neither one spoke, but a silent understanding passed between them. April nodded slightly and smiled, and Lee returned the smile. He patted her on the knee, and then swung into the saddle.

Chapter sixty-three

It was long after midnight by the time Cooper returned with the horses.

Yancy had built a small fire, and he was sitting beside it. Cooper tended to the horses and joined his brother.

Yancy had wrapped his wound, and the rag was soaked with blood.

"How's the arm?" Cooper asked.

"I'll live," Yancy said, and added, "Took you long enough."

"I rode up to two clusters of trees before I found the right cluster."

Yancy smiled faintly.

"Want supper?" Cooper offered. "There's food in the saddlebags."

"Ain't hungry," Yancy shook his head.

"Me neither," Cooper replied. It was silent a moment, and he said, "I reckon we should cook a big supper tomorrow evening. They'll probably be hungry when they ride in."

"Sure might."

"I'm sorta anxious to see how it went."

"Me too."

Cooper nodded, and asked, "Want some coffee?"

Yancy's face lit up.

"I could drink a little."

"Or a lot," Cooper smiled, and said, "I'll make some."

Yancy nodded, and Cooper walked over to No-see-ums and rummaged through the pack.

Chapter sixty-four

To Winchester's surprise, they didn't ride out of the running water for several miles. Once they were on muddy ground, he kicked his horse up to a trot.

The night air was cool, and daylight couldn't arrive fast enough for the soaked, shivering riders.

Brian rode beside Winchester, and he looked concerned.

"Ground sure is slick," he commented.

"Is a little," Winchester agreed.

"But it's better than wading though water," Brian said, and added, "This country can sure flood in a hurry."

"Sure can," Winchester replied. "But, it's just what we needed."

"How's that?"

"It wiped out our tracks," Winchester explained. "Gave us some time."

"Enough time to ride back to Texas?" Brian looked hopeful.

"Not *that* much time. Our best chance is still that hill."

Brian nodded thoughtfully and asked, "How far off is it?"

Winchester thought a moment.

"Long as we don't stop much, we should reach it sometime tomorrow afternoon."

Brian nodded again. A few seconds passed, and he said, "I wonder how Yancy and Cooper made out."

"I'm sure they're fine," Winchester replied. "They're too ornery to die. Especially Yancy."

Brian smiled at that, and it fell silent as they trotted on.

Chapter sixty-five

No Worries was furious.

Apaches hated to be caught by surprise, but that's exactly what had happened. As a result, No Worries had lost nearly half his men.

It was a difficult thing, and No Worries refused to accept it. A deep anger burned inside him, and he was determined to have the last victory.

It was still dark as they circled the pass on horseback. They rode in as close as they could, and then they waited for daylight.

It was a long wait.

As soon as dawn arrived, they searched for tracks. However, there were none to be found. The flooding water had wiped away any sign of them.

No Worries was disappointed, but he refused to show it. They rode east, and they spread out as they looked for sign.

No Worries could only guess which direction the hated whites had gone. If they were soldiers, they would go south towards the army posts. If not, they would probably go east towards Texas.

This seemed more likely. However, No Worries was confused, because he'd received no word from the Apaches at the hill.

They rode several miles, and No Worries halted abruptly.

"Look," he spoke gruffly in Apache and pointed.

In front of them, several hundred yards, was a mule.

The mule didn't see them. He limped slightly, but he still managed to trot with purpose. His head was close to the ground, and he traveled east in a straight line.

No Worries grunted in thought. One of his warriors started to go after him, but No Worries stopped him.

"What do we do?" The warrior, also speaking in Apache, asked with a confused look.

"We follow," No Worries declared.

Part Six
"United Paths"

Chapter sixty-six

Yancy and Cooper couldn't sleep. They finally gave up a few hours before dawn.

Yancy rebuilt the fire, and Cooper cooked breakfast. After they ate, they felt somewhat refreshed. They drank more coffee, and then Cooper unpacked the shovels.

It was easy digging, and it didn't take them long to bury the dead. Afterwards, they grubbed a few mesquite bushes around the base of the hill so they could better defend it.

"You still determined to set this trap?" Yancy asked.

"Yes, unless you have a better idea."

Yancy shook his head.

"Can't think of one."

Cooper nodded, and he looked thoughtful as he studied the country in front of them.

"If you were the Apaches, where would you leave the horses?" He asked.

It was silent as Yancy studied the landscape.

"There," he finally pointed to a low spot several hundred yards away.

"I agree," Cooper said, and they walked over and inspected the area.

It was a likely spot. There was a sand dune between them and the hill, and at the bottom it mushroomed out a bit, making a natural corral of sorts.

"This is the place," Cooper declared, and Yancy nodded his agreement.

There were several thick, thorny shrubs scattered about, and Cooper gestured at two shrubs that were close together.

"There," he said.

Yancy agreed, and Cooper started digging between the two shrubs, being careful not to disturb them.

It was sandy, easy digging, and the two brothers traded out often. They dug the hole about the size of a grave, only shallower.

They were both drenched with sweat by the time they finished. Cooper put the shovel aside, climbed in the hole, pressed himself flat, and glanced up at Yancy.

"What do you think?"

Yancy nodded slowly.

"Should work."

Cooper returned the nod. He climbed out, grabbed the shovel, and glanced at the sun.

"Almost noon," he said. "According to my calculations, they could show up anytime now."

"*Precise* calculations," Yancy reminded.

"Right," Cooper smiled faintly.

"Well, we'd best settle in and keep watch," Yancy suggested.

"Reckon we'd better," Cooper agreed, and they trudged back to the top of the hill.

Chapter sixty-seven

Winchester kept a brisk pace through the night, and by dawn the mountains were far behind them.

The sunlight was a welcome change. It warmed up quickly, and their damp clothes finally dried out.

Winchester pulled up around midmorning. Their horses were exhausted, and soaked with sweat.

"Best let our horses breathe a bit," Winchester suggested, and he looked at the women. "We also have some food if you're hungry."

Everyone nodded and dismounted.

Winchester rummaged through Jeremiah's saddlebags and found a can of peaches. Then, he slipped back down the trail a ways to watch their back trail.

Meanwhile, Lee dug out some hardtack and beef jerky and offered it to Rachel and April.

"Might not taste the best, but it'll have to do until we can stop," he said.

"Tastes just fine to me," April replied as she bit into the tough hardtack.

"Best meal we've had in weeks," Rachel added.

Lee smiled at them, and then he walked over and examined his exhausted mount, as did Rondo and Brian. Meanwhile, Rachel and April sat on the ground a short distance from them.

"Are you doing all right?" April shot Rachel a concerned look.

"Yes, I think so."

April nodded and asked, "Does Rondo know about the baby yet?"

Rachel shook her head.

"No, I haven't told him."

April looked surprised.

"Why not?"

"I've decided to wait," Rachel declared.

"For what?"

"Until we're home," Rachel explained. "He has enough to think about right now. I don't want to startle him. And, I'd like to be alone when I tell him."

"Just don't wait too long," April cautioned.

"I won't," Rachel promised.

April nodded, and they heard a noise from behind. Seconds later, Winchester came trotting up.

"See any Injuns?" Rondo asked from the horses.

"No, but they'll be along," Winchester replied. "We'd best keep going."

Rondo nodded, and everybody moved to their horses and mounted up.

"How close are we to the hill?" Brian asked.

"We'll be there midafternoon," Winchester replied.

He kicked up Jeremiah's horse, and everyone followed.

Chapter sixty-eight

Yancy and Cooper lay stretched out on the ground, on top of the hill, concealed behind bushes. Cooper had his spyglass, and they took turns sweeping the countryside, looking for riders.

It was midafternoon, and the hot sun burned down unmercifully.

"Where are they?" Yancy asked, irritation in his voice.

"They'll be along."

"I'm starting to wonder if we made a bad decision, splitting up like we did."

"Too late now," Cooper replied, and added, "Besides, bad decisions make for good stories."

Yancy snorted at that, it was silent for a bit.

Suddenly, Cooper grunted as he squinted through his eyeglass.

"You see 'em?" Yancy asked.

"I sure do."

"About time," Yancy said softly.

"They're just trotting along, and don't seem to be in any trouble," Cooper commented, and he swept the eyeglass to the west and studied their back trail. "No Injuns that I can see."

"Any sign of Rachel or April?"

Cooper swept his eyeglass back to the riders, and several seconds passed as he squinted through it.

"Yep, I see two females," Cooper announced, excitement in his voice.

Yancy grinned, but didn't say anything.

***

Yancy and Cooper kept a watchful eye as they drew close. Finally, Cooper stood and waved at them.

"Come on in!" He yelled.

They trotted up and halted at the tank. Their thirsty horses drank deeply while Yancy and Cooper walked down the hill.

Several seconds passed while everyone looked at each other, and then Cooper cleared his throat.

"You made it," he said.

"We did," Winchester spoke.

"Any trouble?"

"Some, but we handled it."

"Figured you would," Cooper said, and he glanced at April and Rachel. "You two all right?"

"We're fine," Rachel smiled at him.

Cooper returned the smile.

"Good," he said.

"What happened here?" Rondo spoke up, and he gestured at Yancy's bandaged arm. "Are you hurt?"

"Just a scratch," Yancy replied, and added, "No trouble here. We also have three extra horses."

"I noticed that," Winchester said as he studied the horses.

"Where's Jeremiah?" Yancy asked suddenly.

They glanced at each other, and Rondo cleared his throat.

"He didn't make it," he said softly.

A look of regret crossed Yancy's face. He glanced at Cooper, and he then turned away, his hands on his hips.

Chapter sixty-nine

Cooper rekindled the fire and cooked some salt pork and coffee. Meanwhile, Yancy kept watch while everybody else tended to their horses.

"Come get it," Cooper finally said.

They filled their plates, and they spread out around the top of the hill and kept watch while they ate. It was the best meal they'd had in days, and everyone ate with a vengeance. Afterwards, they refilled their coffee cups.

"So, what's next?" Lee asked as he took a swig of coffee.

"We wait for the Apaches to show up," Winchester replied.

"Why don't we ride out?" Lee replied. "We might be able to outrun 'em."

"No," Winchester said flatly. "We couldn't."

Lee scowled, but Winchester ignored the look.

"You sure they're following you?" Cooper entered the conversation.

"They'll be along," Winchester said with confidence.

It was silent as everyone thought on that, and then they settled in and kept watch.

The afternoon passed slowly. Rachel and April sat under the shade of a tree and took a nap, and everybody else took turns looking through the eyeglass.

About an hour before dark, Yancy suddenly grunted.

"What is it?" Cooper hissed.

A few tense seconds passed, and Yancy shook his head in disbelief.

"It's Jug-head," he announced.

"Jug-head!" Winchester said, surprised. "He was crippled. We had to leave him."

"He ain't now," Yancy replied, and he handed the spyglass to Winchester.

"How 'bout that," Winchester said, pleased. "Good ol' Jug-head."

Neither Yancy nor Cooper replied, and several seconds passed as Winchester squinted through the eyeglass. He swept the countryside, and he sat up abruptly.

"Injuns," he said softly.

"Where?" Yancy demanded.

"'Bout a half mile behind Jug-head. I only caught a glimpse."

Yancy glanced at Cooper and looked back at Winchester.

"Are you suggesting they're following Jug-head?" He asked, disbelief in his voice.

"What it looked like to me," Winchester said.

Everyone was silent as they thought on that.

"And Jug-head's leading them straight to us," Yancy finally said.

"It would appear so," Winchester agreed.

Chapter seventy

"I've never liked that mule," Yancy declared irritably.

"Aw, it ain't his fault," Winchester said. "They'd have found us eventually anyway."

Yancy didn't reply. Instead, he asked, "How many Apaches?"

"About a dozen, give or take."

"You fellows narrowed them down some," Yancy said, surprised.

"We got a few," Winchester nodded.

"But there's still more than us," Lee spoke up.

Yancy looked thoughtful, and they watched as Jug-head trotted up. As soon as he spotted them, he perked his ears and brayed.

"Yes, we hear you," Yancy said sourly.

Jug-head trotted over to the horses and took his place beside No-see-ums. There was no need to tie him; it was obvious he wasn't going anywhere.

Yancy scowled at the mule, and then he glanced at Winchester.

"What do you reckon they'll do next?" He asked.

"You're asking my opinion?" Winchester looked surprised.

Yancy frowned.

"I am."

"Well," Winchester looked thoughtful. "They'll probably wait until dark and ride in as close as they can. Then, they'll surround us on foot and be ready to attack come dawn."

"Sounds reasonable," Yancy agreed. He glanced at Cooper and asked, "Still want to try it?"

"It's worth a shot," Cooper replied.

"Try what?" Winchester asked, confused.

"We set up a trap of sorts," Cooper explained.

"Trap?" Winchester raised a doubtful eye. "What sort of trap?"

"Just watch and learn something," Yancy replied curtly.

Chapter seventy-one

"I'll be right back," Yancy said, and he and Cooper stood.

"You're going out there?" Winchester frowned his disapproval.

"That's right," Yancy said. "Everybody else stay put and keep a sharp lookout."

Winchester wanted to object, but he remained silent.

Before they left, Cooper grabbed a saddle blanket. Winchester wondered what it was for, but he didn't ask as they slipped out.

They worked their way down the hill, crossed the sand dune, and arrived at the hole.

Cooper crawled in, and he held his rifle beside him.

"Ready?" Yancy asked, and Cooper nodded.

Yancy worked quickly. He placed the saddle blanket over Cooper's head and back, and he scooped up handfuls of sand and covered the blanket. Then, he spread out the remaining sand over Cooper's legs.

Next, he pulled out his knife and slashed the roots of a nearby greasewood. He swept the area clean of any tracks or disturbance.

Yancy stood back and observed his work. Everything was covered and concealed, and he grunted his satisfaction.

"You all right under there?" Yancy asked.

"Just lovely."

"How does it feel?"

"Sandy."

"Don't suffocate," Yancy warned.

"Hold on," Cooper replied.

Moving slow so he wouldn't disturb anything, Cooper pushed a stick up beside the blanket. He pulled it back, and it left a tiny hole in the sand.

"See that hole?" Cooper asked.

Yancy shook his head.

"I can't tell if you just shook your head," Cooper replied after a moment of silence.

Yancy scowled.

"I don't see anything," he said.

"Good, now I can breath," Cooper replied.

"I'm glad you're comfortable."

"I wouldn't go that far."

Yancy smiled, and said, "Well, I'd best get back up there. Be careful."

"I'll try."

"And remember; this was your idea."

"Thanks."

"I'll see you in a bit."

"I hope so."

Yancy took careful steps backward. He dragged the greasewood behind him and covered his tracks as best he could.

He made his way back to the top of the hill, and Winchester gave him a questioning look.

"Where's Cooper?"

"I left him in a hole," Yancy said, and then he explained.

It was silent as everyone thought on that.

"This might actually work," Winchester grudgingly admitted.

"Glad you like it," Yancy said, and added, "We need to be ready to ride. Best keep your horses saddled."

Everyone nodded in agreement.

Yancy glanced at the lowering sun, and then he settled in behind a shrub and looked out at the countryside.

"Now comes the hard part," he said softly.

"What's that?" Rondo asked.

"Waiting."

Chapter seventy-two

Night settled over their camp. Yancy kicked out the fire, and darkness surrounded them.

An hour passed, but it felt longer.

Especially for Yancy. He looked anxious, and Lee watched him for a moment.

"You worried?" Lee finally asked.

"About what?" Yancy glanced at him.

"Coop."

Yancy thought about denying it, but then shrugged.

"A little."

"Cooper knows what he's doing," Lee tried to be helpful.

"So did the boys at the Alamo," Yancy replied.

Lee smiled faintly. A few seconds passed, and he chuckled.

"What is it?" Yancy asked.

"Oh, I was just thinking."

"There's a first time for everything."

Lee shot Yancy a dark look.

"So, what's on your mind?" Yancy asked after a moment.

"Nothing much. I just realized something."

"And what's that?"

"Since this all started, you and I haven't had even one argument."

Yancy looked thoughtful. He nodded and glanced at Winchester.

"I've had other things on my mind, is all," he explained.

Lee glanced at Winchester and smiled knowingly.

***

Another hour came and went.

It was still, and very quiet. There were no frogs croaking this night, or anything else. There was only an eerie silence, and everyone felt anxious.

"How much longer?" Rondo whispered.

"Anytime now," Yancy replied.

Rondo nodded, and then he said, "There's one thing I can't figure."

"What's that?" Lee looked over at him.

"Who was that woman Yancy and Cooper found a few weeks back?"

"Been wondering that myself," Brian entered the conversation.

Rondo glanced at Rachel, who was close beside him.

"Were there any other captives?" He asked.

"One," she replied. "Her name was Lucy. No Worries killed her when she tried to escape."

Everyone was startled.

"Lucy Nash?" Yancy hissed.

"She never mentioned her last name," Rachel replied. "But, she was arrogant and very foolish."

"Sure sounds like her," Lee said wryly.

"What did she look like?" Yancy urged.

Rachel thought a moment.

"She was short, pretty, and had curly, blond hair."

"That's her," Lee declared, and Rondo and Brian nodded their agreement.

"I reckon she finally got what she deserved," Brian said.

"How about that," Lee said softly, and he glanced at Yancy. "Looks like you don't have to worry about arresting her."

"It would appear so," Yancy agreed.

Chapter seventy-three

Cooper was soaked with sweat by the time the sun finally went down, and then he got slightly cold as the night air chilled. But he didn't allow himself to shiver; he couldn't take the chance of disrupting the sand.

Time passed painfully slow, and Cooper remained perfectly still.

He sensed, rather than heard, when the Apaches finally arrived. He listened intently, and he finally picked up the sound of horses moving toward him.

His body was tense, but he didn't move a muscle. He could tell they were close, and unrecognizable Apache words reached his ears.

There were footsteps, and Cooper gripped his rifle as they passed by only a few feet from him.

After that he heard an occasional stomping of the feet from the Indian ponies, but that was all.

He wondered if a guard had been left. If there were, he would have to silence him.

Cooper continued to lie still, and he counted the time in his head. After what seemed forever, he finally nodded to himself.

It was time.

Moving slowly, he pushed upwards. He crawled out from under the saddle blanket, and sand caved in around him.

Cooper didn't move as his eyes adjusted to the darkness, and then he took a slow, careful look around.

The Indian ponies were tethered together not far away. He didn't see any Indians, and he grunted softly in satisfaction.

With his rifle in hand, he crawled toward the ponies. He stood to full height as he got close.

Suddenly, he heard a surprised grunt behind him. He spun around, and he recognized No Worries. He stood between the two shrubs, and he held the saddle blanket.

No Worries spotted Cooper at the same instant, and recognition flashed in his eyes.

"Landon," he said in thick, broken English.

Before No Worries could move, Cooper swung his rifle up and cocked the hammer. But he hesitated to fire, because a shot would alert the other Apaches.

No Worries understood this, and he grunted. He ran toward Cooper, his tomahawk in hand.

Cooper un-cocked his rifle and leaped forward to meet the challenge.

The nimble Apache covered ground fast. He swung his tomahawk, but Cooper dove to the ground and rolled as No Worries' momentum carried him past Cooper.

Cooper sprang to his feet and spun around. Swinging his rifle as a club, he aimed for the Apache's head.

No Worries was spinning around as Cooper's blow hit him in the face. It was a violent impact, and Cooper almost dropped his rifle.

There was a crunching sound, and blood spurted from No Worries' mouth. Cooper heard a gurgling sound, and No Worries dropped and didn't move.

Cooper didn't wait around. He hurried to the Indian ponies, and his knife flashed as he cut them loose.

He held on to the last horse. He jumped on his back, and he fired his rifle up into the air.

His horse was startled, but Cooper managed to hang on. The other Indian ponies broke and ran, and they went west towards the mountains.

Cooper grinned as he loped behind them, pushing them on.

Chapter seventy-four

Even though they were expecting it, everyone still jumped when the rifle shot sounded out.

"All right; let's go!" Yancy said tersely.

They stood, moved to their horses, and mounted up. Yancy led Cooper's horse, Lee led No-see-ums, and Brian led the extra horse.

"What about Jug-head?" Winchester asked.

"Leave him!" Yancy replied curtly.

Winchester nodded regretfully and kicked up his horse. He left the hill in a dead run, and everyone followed.

Winchester spotted an Apache racing towards them as he attempted to cut them off.

He reached down, pulled out his rifle, and charged towards him.

The Apache also held a rifle, and he started to take aim. However, as Winchester rode by, he took aim and fired from the hip. There was a loud thumping sound, and the Apache did a flip in the air and landed on his back.

Rachel, April, Lee, Brian, Rondo, and Yancy were close behind Winchester. They kept their horses in a dead run for several miles, and then Yancy called out for everybody to stop.

"Everyone all right?" Yancy asked.

Everyone was breathless as they nodded.

Yancy returned the nods and glanced at Winchester.

"You're handy with that rifle," he commented.

Winchester smiled.

"That's why they call me Winchester."

"Now what?" Rondo spoke up.

"We wait for Cooper," Yancy replied.

"What if he doesn't show up?" Lee asked.

"He will," Yancy declared.

They waited in tense silence. Half an hour passed, and everyone became restless.

They finally heard a noise, and everyone gripped their firearm. But then they recognized Cooper as he came trotting up out of the darkness. Behind him, he led Jughead.

"Look what I found!" He grinned.

Everyone but Yancy returned the grin.

"Why'd you bring him along?" Yancy scowled.

"Injuns already followed him once," Cooper pointed out.

Yancy couldn't argue with that, so he changed the subject.

"You all right?"

"Got some sand in my britches, but I'll live."

"I can imagine," Yancy said, and asked, "Have any trouble?"

"Not much. But, I did have an interesting conversation with No Worries."

"Oh?" Yancy raised an eyebrow.

"He even knew who I was. Called me Landon."

"What happened?"

"'Bout what you'd expect. He tried to kill me, but I didn't let him."

"No Worries is dead?" Winchester entered the conversation.

"It's possible," Cooper replied. "If not, they might have to rename him No Teeth."

"You didn't make sure?" Winchester frowned his disapproval.

"I was busy."

Winchester looked disappointed. It was quiet, and he asked, "But you managed to run off their horses?"

"Yep," Cooper nodded. "Those ponies are halfway back to the mountains by now."

A relieved look crossed everyone's face.

"I suggest we put some more miles between them and us," Winchester suggested. "Just 'cause they're horseless doesn't mean they won't make one last attempt. Apaches can travel fast, even on foot."

"Let's go then," Yancy said.

Cooper switched back to his horse, and they left out in a brisk trot.

Epilogue

They kept up the pace until dawn, and only then did they stop.

Everybody dismounted, and they dug in their saddlebags and pulled out some canned goods. They took small sips from their canteens while they ate.

Everyone was in a cheerful mood. Lee and April kept glancing at each other, as did Rondo and Rachel. The only person that looked slightly remorseful was Yancy.

"What's the matter?" Cooper glanced at him.

"Jeremiah," he said somberly. "He deserved better."

Everyone nodded, and there was a moment of silence as they thought on him.

"He was a good man," Rondo finally said.

"He tried," Yancy replied, and he glanced at Winchester. "You might as well keep his horse. You need one."

"'Preciate it," Winchester replied. He took one more swig from his canteen and stood. "Well, I'd best be on my way. I've a report to make, and I'm long overdue."

"I appreciate your help," Rondo spoke up.

"It's what us Landons do," Winchester grinned, and he glanced at everybody else. "Adios," he said.

Everybody nodded back.

"Winchester," Yancy said, his voice stern. "Take care of yourself."

"Always," Winchester smiled his boyish smile.

"I have a feeling we'll be seeing you again, real soon."

"We *should* keep in touch. After all, we're family."

"We'll plan on it," Yancy smiled tightly.

"Well, be seeing you," Winchester waved his hand.

"Yes, you will," Yancy said softly.

Winchester stepped into the saddle and kicked up his horse, and everybody stood there and watched him. He slowly became a blur and disappeared in the distance.

Yancy turned and looked briefly at everyone.

First, he glanced at Rondo and Rachel. They were holding hands, and Yancy noticed that Rachel's other hand was resting on her stomach. She had a knowing smile, but Rondo wasn't aware.

Yancy frowned in thought as he turned his attention to Lee and April. They stood side by side, and April rested her head on his shoulder. As for Brian, he was watching them with a pleased look on his face.

Yancy looked at his brother last, and Cooper's eyes twinkled back at him.

Yancy gave everyone a satisfying smile of a job well done.

"Let's go home," he said.

About the Author

Born in West Texas, Tell Cotten is a seventh generation Texan. He comes from a family with a ranching heritage and is a member of the Sons of the Republic of Texas. Besides writing, he is also in the cattle business, and he resides in West Texas with his wife, Andi, and their two children.

Tell has enjoyed writing from an early age, and he also has a great love of the history of the west. WARPATH is his eighth novel in The Landon Saga series.

For announcements of new releases and all other information, please like The Landon Saga Page on Facebook https://www.facebook.com/TheLandonSaga Or, you can join The Landon Saga Fan Group https://www.facebook.com/groups/784798154926122/ You can also visit Tell Cotten's website http://tellcotten.wordpress.com/

Acknowledgements

I would like to thank my wife and my family for all their help and support. Without them this wouldn't be possible. I'd also like to thank God for the gift of writing.

Special thanks goes out to Bill for the fantastic drawing, and thanks to Mike and Marcy for putting the cover together.

And lastly, I'd like to thank Melissa for all her advice, help, and hard work.

Enjoy this excerpt from Tell Cotten's upcoming novel:

Fastest Gun Around
Book nine in The Landon Saga series

He was a thin, tall, and lanky old-timer. He had sharp, narrow eyes, and a white beard. There was also the suggestion of lost handsomeness in his face.

He held a doubled barreled shotgun over his saddle. The hammers were pulled back, and both barrels were pointed at me.

I swallowed uneasily.

"You make one move toward that Colt, and I'll blast you from here to Mexico," he said in a curt, harsh voice.

"I won't."

"Who are you?" He demanded.

"Rondo Landon."

He grunted at that. I saw a hint of admiration in his eyes, but there was also some hostility.

"Heard of you."

"Most have."

"You as good with that Colt as they say you are?"

"Pretty much."

"Fastest gun around, eh?"

"I wouldn't put it like that."

"I heard you betrayed your gang and went honest."

"Not exactly how it happened," I frowned. "But, I am honest."

He gestured at the dun horse.

"If you're so trustworthy, why are you riding somebody else's horse?"

"How'd you know that?"

"I was watching from the ridge through my spyglass," he said. "You took him without permission."

"Nobody was home," I explained. "But, I pinned a note on the door."

"Sure you did."

"Let's ride back and see," I said, irritation rising in my voice.

"I did, but there was no note."

I frowned in confusion.

"It must have blown off," I said, and added, "I explained everything."

"How 'bout explaining it again."

I hesitated, but then I told him what happened. His face was emotionless while he listened.

"Sounds reasonable," he said after I had finished.

I breathed a sigh of relief. However, he didn't lower the shotgun or un-cock it, and that worried me.

"You don't believe me?" I asked.

"Sure."

"Then why don't you ease those hammers back down," I suggested.

He chuckled gruffly.

"Making you nervous?"

"Just a bit," I admitted.

"I haven't told you who I am yet."

"Oh?"

"For three, long years I've yearned for this moment, meeting you face to face."

"Glad I could help."

He seemed to be enjoying this confrontation, but he was the only one.

"My name's Gage," he announced. "Gage Palmer."

The name meant nothing to me.

"Nice to meet you," I said.

He didn't reply, and he watched me closely.

Several tense seconds passed.

A thought suddenly occurred to me, and I felt a jolt of surprise. I looked into his eyes, and he smiled smugly.

"Did you say *Palmer*?" I asked.

"I did."

"Any relation to a Ryan Palmer?"

He nodded slightly.

"He was my son."

We were quiet as we thought on that.

"Oh, boy," I finally murmured.

"And you killed him," he said, and there was anger in his voice.

Coming soon from Solstice Publishing

For announcements of new releases and all other information, please like The Landon Saga Page on Facebook https://www.facebook.com/TheLandonSaga or you can join The Landon Saga Facebook group https://www.facebook.com/groups/784798154926122/

www.ingramcontent.com/pod-product-compliance
Lightning Source LLC
Chambersburg PA
CBHW060937180626
46817CB00004B/1602